LEESA HARKER is from Belfast and studied English Language and Literature at the Open University. She has been a bank manager, car mechanic, perfume spritzer at Debenhams and an animal welfare officer at the USPCA – but always dreamed of being a writer. Those dreams came true when her books *Fifty Shades of Red White and Blue* and *Dirty Dancin in le Shebeen* were published in 2012 and became instant bestsellers across Northern Ireland. A hugely successful adaptation of *Fifty Shades of Red White and Blue* was staged in Belfast in 2013.

To find out more about Leesa and her work visit
www.leesaharker.com
or follow her on Twitter @leesaharker

G000138626

Maggie's Feg Run

Leesa Harker

·THE·
BLACK
·STAFF·
PRESS

First published in 2013 by Blackstaff Press
4c Heron Wharf
Sydenham Business Park
Belfast BT3 9LE
with the assistance of
The Arts Council of Northern Ireland

Printed and bound by CPI Group UK (Ltd), Croydon CRO 4YY

A CIP catalogue for this book is available
from the British Library

ISBN 978 0 85640 907 3

www.leesaharker.com
www.blackstaffpress.com

For Sylvia Jackson
Always missed at the C&C

Contents

1

A sausage, two chicken balls and an accumulator bet

Well. It all started when Big Sally-Ann's da won big at le bookies. Sure me an Big Sally-Ann were sittin in her house watchin *Jeremy Kyle* reruns, back-til-back. Ler was two brothers buckin le same woman, and a man wih one eye and no teeth gettin his head dug in by some head-the-ball woman wih 'CONT' tattooed on her forehead. Len ler was a wee divvy woman who was goin til America til marry a man on death row. Fuckin binlid. Big Jeremy was givin it stacks til her like, but sure she was dead from le neck up. Eejit.

Me an Big Sally-Ann'd had a wick few months an we were lyin low. Big Sally-Ann had drapped

1

Igor le dogger when she found out he'd a wife an ten kids back in Transylvania. Sure he was wantin her til move over ler and become wife number two. Here bes her, 'No chance sunny Jim'. Like she was gutted for a wee while and she gat a real sickener about men. But len she bucked a wee lad from Carrick out le back a Ownies one night an lat tuck her mind right off it. Here bes her, 'Like I was gettin fed up buckin outside til be hanast, Maggot. It's no fun in le winter – sure I'd chilblains on my diddies an everythin.'

An me an Big Billy Scriven had had a massive ding-dong one night in le shebeen, after I found out he'd bucked thon swamp donkey Gretta 'Grotbegs' Gilmore behind my back. Sure he'd denied it an all but it was written all over his pasty bake. Big Gretta had telled everybady – half le friggin shebeen knew about it before I did. I was that affronted I near killed him. Bate him over le head wih Ricky 'Rangers' Mason's flute an he'd til get three stitches – I was like a batein bear. So, I hadn't spoke til him in weeks. Which is harder lan it sounds because our wee Road is small like. Ya can't avoid anybady for too long.

Anyhie, back til Big Sally-Ann's da – he

pulled up in a taxi while we were lyin on le sofa watchin King Kyle. He run in that quick, his foot was through le front door an his arse was still in le taxi. If le DLA had have seen him ler woulda been a Stewards' Enquiry about it. Even though he only has one leg, he sure can move when he wants til! Sure I thought he was havin a pure cardiac or somethin le way he was waving his arms about an shoutin an all.

Here bes him, 'Sally-Ann, Maggie, I've hit le jackpot! Le jackpot! An accumulator bet came through for me. Fuckin luckiest bastard on le Road le day! Pure fluke like!'

Here's me, 'Whaaa?'

Here's Big Sally-Ann, 'You're jokin me, Da – hie much?'

Here's him, 'Two grand, love, and change!' Nen he lucked around le room an whispered, 'Is your ma still out?'

Here bes Big Sally-Ann, 'Awye. Down at le butchers gettin your Friday night sausages in.'

Here bes him, 'Tell her it was fifteen hundred just. But here, fuck le sausages, love – we're goin down til le all-you-can-eat Chinese buffet in Yorkgate!'

An, God love him, he did take us down an treated us all til dinner wih his winnins. Sure le wee Chinese waiter near died when he saw le size a Big Sally-Ann. I'm sure he was thinkin, fuck ler goes our profits for le night – thon big girl's gonna ate all round her! An we all did like. Sure I near had til get rolled outta le place. Lat's le thing wih Chinese food, ya shovel it in lat quick, ya don't realise hie much yer actually atein. Sure I had enough ribs on my plate til build a stepladder. Big Sally-Ann's ma sat down wih a bowl a deep-fried seaweed.

Here bes her, 'Lat's le best thing about in here, ya can try a wee bit of everything like. Go continental.'

Here bes me, 'Awye like le pick 'n' mix at Woolies.'

Here's her da, 'What in le name a God's lat ler on yer plate? It lucks like burnt grass!'

Here's her ma, 'It's seaweed – deep fried. It's a delicacy in China like. I saw it on le Discovery Channel.' Like Big Sally-Ann's ma had gat Sky in an her bax chipped – sure she was watchin all lese weird channels an all.

Here's her da, 'Sheep's dick is a delicacy in

4

Timbuktu – doesn't mean I'm gonna champ on one in le all-you-can-eat fuckin buffet!'

But Big Sally-Ann's ma gat stuck in – I don't think she liked it much but she woulden give in an admit it.

Well, by le time we were on our seconds, Big Sally-Ann's ma near had le two grand spent in her head. Sure she had curtains an carpets bought, an a trip til Menarys for a new frock planned. Her da near choked on his chicken ball when she mentioned her chum Minnie's whirlpool bath. But here, len I had an idea.

Here bes me, 'Here, have ya ever heard of le sayin, speculate til accumulate?'

Here's everybady, 'Naaaaa.'

Here's me, 'What wih Doris here spendin yer two grand in Harry Corry on le Road, hie about ya try til grow it a bit? Like invest it?'

Here bes Big Sally-Ann, 'What wih le current economic climate, investin's a risky business, chum.'

We all lucked at her wih open mouths. We sat in silence as a deep-fried seaweed ball rolled across le floor.

Nen she gat all flustered an here's her, 'Oh I

think I've had one duck pancake too many, it's goin til my head – I'm talkin like a pastie supper! I'm nat watchin lat CNN channel no more. It's like brainwashin me!'

Here bes me, 'Luck, me an you's been wantin til head to Benidorm on a feg run for ages nie. What about if we barra a grand off yer da, head to Spain an nen we can pay him back – wih interest – and make money for ourselves too. It's like a wee bidda pure genius like!'

Here's Big Sally-Ann, 'Fuck me Maggot, lat's a cracker idea!'

But Big Sally-Ann's da wasn't too sure about it. Sure he was ascared of us drinkin le lat an comin back wih nathin but sunburn an a dose of le clap. But, in le end, me an Big Sally-Ann managed til talk him round. I gat til workin out le finance of it all, cos Big Sally-Ann was busy eyein up le wee waiter. God love him he was five-futt-nathin an sweatin like a nun at a stag do. She was starin at him – lickin a battered sausage an winkin at him an all. So, I said til her da lat we would pay back le grand an go halfers on le profits, an here's him, 'Right ya be Maggie – nie I'm countin on you til nat piss lis money up le wall – do ya hear me?'

Here bes her ma, 'Nie I'm tellin yez, yez better nat go buck daft over ler. Ley throw girls like yous intil jail for flashin yer boobs an all in lem countries. I seen it on le Discovery Channel.'

Here bes me, 'Ack, Doris – ya wanna lay off lem documentaries, chum – watch a bidda le *O.C.* or somethin.'

Here's her, 'What's lat when yer at home like?'

Here's me, '*Orange County* – like California in America. It's all about rich women wih fake diddies an all – it's pure beezer like.'

Here's her, 'Ack, I'd rather watch a documentary on Orange County Antrim – friggin Yanks think they know it all. Need ler heads lucked at wih a hammer.' Nen she smiles an ler's seaweed hangin out between every tooth.

Here's me, 'Awye.' Nen I lucks at Big Sally-Ann an sure she's sneaked over til le wee waiter. Nie, I dunno what she was sayin, but she was holdin a plate under his nose an on it was a sausage an two chicken balls in le shape of a big dick. Sure le wee lawd lucked like he was about til bust out gernin. Ya can take thon big girl nowhere – an I was about til take her til le

7

biggest buckin ground on le planet – Benidorm! Here's me til myself, a haliday's just what le dacter ordered for me an le big girl. We'd laid low for long enough – it was time til do a bidda partyin, Belfast-style. Like ya can't keep an old dog down. We were both free, single an ready til fumble. And it was about time I gat le Muff an airin. Big Sally-Ann slides back over til le wee table after le waiter run away an here's me, 'Bring it on til fuck, Sally-Ann! Benidorm – here we come! Get 'er bucked! Yeeeeooowwwwww!'

2

Grotbegs is up le spout

Well, le next day, we went down til le travel agents on le Road, til see what we cud book. Some stuck-up wee hoor-beg, wih drew-on eyebrows an her diddies hangin out her half-washed V neck, was sittin filin her nails. Nen she rolled her eyes at us an says, 'Can I help yez?'

Here's me, 'Awye – ya can.' An I sat down. Like she lucked at us like she thought we'd no money. So, here's me, 'Luckin a wee trip til Benidorm, love. Cheap as possible, central til le bars an all like.'

Nen here bes her, 'Well, it's not cheap anymore – there's taxes for flights and airports and the bags are expensive now too.' Well here's me til myself, lis wee bi-atch is wantin rid of us so she

9

can get on wih filin her nails or textin some wee lawd. So, I tuck le thousand quid outta my beg an I wallaped it down on le table in front of her.

Here's me, 'Thousand quid ler. Nie we need til keep a few hundred for fegs – but aside from lat, work away.' Well, her eyes lit up. She smelt commission – she was typin away on le computer like a tramp on chips. So, we were sittin waitin til see what she came up with, when I hears a rap at le shap windee. Sure it was Big Gretta Grotbegs Gilmore. Here's me, 'Whaaa?'

Nen she shouts through le windee, 'Mere out. I want ye!' So here bes me til Big Sally-Ann, 'Don't you book nathin til I get back like. Right?'

Here's her, 'Awye, Maggot. Here, do ya want me til come out an get yer back in case she wallaps ye?'

Here's me, 'Naaa chum, I can handle thon.' So, I stepped out an lit a feg. Like, I'd no beef wih Grotbegs. She bucked Big Billy while he was seein me but he's le one I wanted til knack le melt outta – nat her.

Here bes Gretta, 'Maggie. Me an Billy's makin a go of it.'

Here's me, 'Awye. An whaaa?'

Here's her, 'Stay le fuck outta his life or I'll do ye in.'

Here's me, 'Ha-whaaa? Are you touched, love? I coulden give a flyin fuck about his life. He made his bed – nie he can buck you in it … for all le good lat'll do him. Nie take yerself off til fuck, will ya?'

Like ya wanna seen le staunch of her. Standin ler wih her ten bellies.

Here bes her, 'Aye, well he prefers my bed til yours.'

Nen here's me til myself, oh lis is fightin talk. So, I goes til grab her by le scruff an she steps back an shouts all over le Road, 'I'm pregnant! I'm pregnant! An it's Billy's. We're gonna be a family an we don't want le likes of an auld hoor like you tryin til break us up.' Well. My feg dropped outta my mouth, an I just stood ler gawkin at her. Big Billy had gat Gretta Grotbegs Gilmore pregnant. Fuck me thon kid was gonna luck like a Cabbage Patch doll. But sure I was stunned. I coulden say nathin. I was actually speechless for le first time in donkeys. Doin a line wih him was one thing, but a baby?

Here bes Gretta, 'Bookin a wee haliday?

11

Don't come fuckin back.' Nen she stomped off up le Road.

Well, I went back intil le travel agents an sat down. Big Sally-Ann was talkin away til le wee doll, an I wasn't even listenin. I just nodded nie an again. Like I didden think I was annoyed about Grotbegs bein up le spout. But I had an ache in my chest – or was it my belly? Coulden decide where it was but it was achin all right. I was imaginin Big Billy pushin a wee baby up le Road in its pram, nen down at le swings wih a wee toddler, len kickin a ball about Woodvale Park wih a wee boy. I was sure it was what he'd always wanted, an I suppose I shoulda been happy for him. But I knew it wud mean le end of me an him … forever. Billy wud stick by le mammy of his kid – lat I knew for sure. Even if she did have a face like a full skip (it wud sour milk, I tell ye).

'That's it all booked girls – hope you have a fab time in Benidorm!' I was shook out of my trance by Big Sally-Ann jumpin up an down on le spat like a lunatic.

Here's me, 'Whaaa? Booked? Whaaa?'

Here's Big Sally-Ann, 'Ack, it was too good of

12

a deal til let go – I just booked it!'

Here's me, 'I told ye til wait til I came back, ya dope! Hie much did ya spend?'

Nen le wee doll coughs an gets up, an here bes her, 'I'll just get you a courtesy pen and travel wallet.'

Here's me, 'Ya can shove yer courtesy travel wallet up yer jam roll, love. Get back here nie. Hie much did ya sting my eejit chum for?'

Nen here bes her, 'Now, I'm not paid til take abuse off customers. It was a good deal and she had le cash.'

Here's me, 'Hie much?'

Here's her, 'Nine hundred and fifty pounds.'

Well, I let a yell outta me, 'Whaaaaaaa? I said Benidorm nat fuckin Barbados!'

Here's her, 'I told you it's not as cheap as before – the prices have gone up.'

Here's me, 'Gone up? Gone up? Ya can get a friggin two-bedroom house in le estate for less lese days! Ya've fleeced us, chum!'

Nen here's Big Sally-Ann, 'Ya get free table tennis an all in le hotel. An ler's water aerobics, an free food an drink an all. It'll be pure beezer like, chum.'

Here's me, 'An since when do you fuckin play table tennis?'

Here's her, 'Well I was always good at rounders in school like.'

Here's me, 'One prablam meathead – if we've spent le guts of le grand, hie le fuck are we gonna buy le fegs? Eh?'

Here's her, 'Oh.'

Nen here's me, 'Wise le bap, chum.' Nen I lucks at le wee doll. 'Cancel it, love, we need a cheaper hotel.'

Here's her, 'It's non-refundable. If you cancel, you lose the money.'

Well, I was about til ram her nail file up her exfoliated arse when Big Sally-Ann says, 'Sure we've a whole week, Maggot – we can get up another couple a hundred quid I'm sure.'

Here's me, 'Are you dotin, chum? Sure we coulden even get a tenner up on Saturday night for two kebabs and a tin of Irn Bru between us!'

Here's her, 'Jobs. We'll get jobs.' Well, I bust out laughin. Jobs – imagine! Sure we hadn't worked since 1994 when we gat jobs in le Spar on le Road. Big Sally-Ann gat le sack le first week cos she was linin baxes a Tampax up on

14

le shelves for three hours one night. Sure she has wild OCD when she's in confined spaces. Ya wanna see what she done thon time she gat lacked in le Shebeen overnight. Le place was spatless le next day – ya coulda ate yer Ulster fry off le toilet floor. An lat's sayin somethin. An I gat le sack for nickin fegs. Like I woulda gat away wih it … only le owner walked in on me an wee Dodger Drennan havin a sneaky buck in le storeroom one night. Nie, it wasn't le fact I was gettin rid, it was le fact lat, as Dodger groped my diddie, a bax a ten Lambert an Butler fell outta my chest pocket an on til le floor. So lat was lat. Me, Big Sally-Ann an jobs was a recipe for disaster. But sure, as fate wud have it, we were saunterin on back up le Road an we passed le chippy – an sure what was in le windee? A big sign sayin, JOB VACANCIES. Big Sally-Ann lucked at me, an I lucked at her. Nen in we went.

Well, ler was one vacancy on fryin an one for a bouncer. Well, nat really a bouncer. Ley needed somebady til go round in le car wih le delivery driver, in case he gat robbed. Sure ley were gettin robbed every other night by le same wee gang a hoodies down in le estate. Wee friggers. So, of course, ley tuck one luck at Big Sally-Ann, six foot wih hands like shovels, an she gat le job of Delivery Man's Bodyguard. I gat stuck on fryin duty. We didden bather lettin on lat we were away til Benidorm le fallowin week like – sure I was plannin on skimmin le takins, an gettin all my grub free for le week. An if le owner Nelly Lemon knew I was off on a lilty, she'd be watchin me like a hawk.

So, lat night, me an Big Sally-Ann sat in my flat listenin til Bob Marley an drinkin Buckey. Here bes Big Sally-Ann, 'What did Grotbegs want ye for le day?'

Here's me, 'Ya don't wanna know, chum.'

Here's her, 'A do – or a woulden of asked ye, ya plum.' So, I told her about Grotbegs havin Billy's baby, an lat she told me til fack away off an nat come back from Benidorm. Here's Big Sally-Ann, 'Sleekit bastard. Sure ya didden want him anyway – ye've been messin about wih him for years nie. Cut an run, Maggot. Ler's plenty more flies round le shite, chum.'

Here's me, 'Awye.' An I tuck a swig of Buckey til drown le wee niggle in my belly again. But Big Sally-Ann knew me too well. Here bes her,

'Fuck 'em, chum. Shower a shites ley are.' An she grabbed me round le neck an near squeezed le life outta me. Big eejit. So, we ended up blootered an singin 'No Woman, No Cry' til about four in le mornin. Like we just had til go til work wih hangovers – it was le law! We had our street cred an all til think about!

Nen, as I was driftin off intil a stocious sleep, I thought, frig I feel a bit like important. Like, lis was le end of an era. We weren't gonna be bored housewives (without le bell-end husbands) no more. We were workers. Earnin a crust at le local chippy. Doin le double like, but sure lat's nat le point. I thought til myself, let Big Billy play happy families wih thon swamp donkey. I'm movin on too … startin wih a big blow-out in Benidorm – ya don't get free table tennis in le maternity ward, do ye? Mugs! An I fell asleep huggin my Paris Hilton duvet intil me like le it was le first night I gat it.

3

Workin girls
(doin le double like)

Well, le first day in le chippy was a total disaster.
Sure I had le bokes from eight a'clack lat mornin
– I coulden even hold down a bidda potata bread
wih brown sauce an lat's my favourite hangover
cure. Big Sally-Ann was no better.

Here bes her, 'My head's splittin, chum. Lem
Buckey cacktails wih le tequila in lem was what
done it – we're gonna die le day!' But we somehie
managed til make it down le Road til le chippy
for two a'clack. Big Sally-Ann was out straight
away wih wee Bananaman, le delivery driver.
No wonder he gat robbed all le time, sure he was
a big dope – nat le full shillin like. Well, sure

I thought I'd be standin takin orders, 'What's yours, love?' and, 'Want yer bap buttered, love?' … but no. Wee Nazi Nelly had me scrubbin le floors out le back. Fuck it was rattan. Covered in grease. Even le mice were skatin on it. Nelly's sister Sadie Le Sadist was standin at le back door smokin a feg an watchin me. I felt like Cinder-fuckin-ella wih le two ugly sisters. It was pure hell. Le smell of fish and grease was turnin me somethin shackin. An I was already near ready til batter somebody's face in le fryer when I hears her. Gretta Grotbegs Gilmore.

'Well-done fish, love, an a portion of onion rings. Billy, get yer wallet out!' Sure I jookied round le doorway an ler ley were. Big Billy was well and truly under le thumb there. He was skutterin around her like she was delicate china le stupid eejit. I heard Nazi Nelly askin hie far on she was an Grotbegs said, 'Near about til drop, love.' Well. I was pure ragin. Billy musta been doin a line wih her for ages behind my back if she was near due. An I actually believed lat wee frigger loved me. Hie thick was I? Nen I thought about le other man lat had grabbed my attention around about lat time. Mr Red White

19

and Blue. Awye, he was a schizo and wanted til smack le hole off me. But at least he was hanast about it. Ya knew what ya gat on his tin. Nen, I went til go to le bog an here's Sadie le Sadist, 'Here Maggie, get lem floors finished before ya take yer break.' An she tuck a big dreg of her feg an smiled at me. Well wih her black hair greased back an le grey roots, she lucked like a mix between a skunk an Cruella De-Ville.

Here's me, 'Pish stap, love. Ya can't hold what ya haven't gat in yer hand like. Back in a minute.' So, I went intil le bogs an I thought til myself, no Maggie, yer nat givin up. Get le money, go til Benidorm, get yer head showered an have a fuckin ball – stick it out. So, I waited til le coast was clear, an I sauntered on out an gat stuck intil scrubbin le floor again.

Well, later on lat night, Big Sally-Ann came back til le chippy til take her break. Here bes her, 'Isn't lis great? We're gettin paid for lis shit! Me an Davy's drivin about listenin til nineties rave music!'

Here's me, 'Oh, "Davy" nie is it? On first name terms? Yer tellin me yer drivin about havin a ball wih wee Bananaman, an I'm stuck

20

in here scrubbin floors an gettin orders from Tweedle-Dum an Tweedle-Dee. Fuckin great.' Like even Wee Bananaman's ma didden call him Davy, frig's sake.

Here's her, 'Ack Maggot, come on, think about it. It'll be worth it in le end.' Nen 'Davy' comes in an winks at Big Sally-Ann. Here bes him, ''Mon love, next order's out.' An here bes me til myself, oh awye, she's nobbin le delivery driver. An I imagined lem fallin in love in le wee Ford Mondeo, drivin through Shankill Estate wih le waft of pasties and curry sauce in le air. Nen I realises lat I'd been sniffin Cillit Bang all day, an I was high as a kite. So, at le end of le shift, I gat a fish supper, which turned out til be mostly batter, an nat even one chance til skim some money from le till. Overall … fail. But Big Sally-Ann had a different story til tell. Sure she ended up buckin Bananaman in le back of his car on tap of le last lat of takeaways. Here bes her, 'Frig Maggot, it's been a while. I didden even lumber him – I just spread em an telled him til hurry up.'

Here bes me. 'Frig yer every man's dream, chum.'

Here bes her, 'Awye, but I was lyin on a half-wrapped steakette an my arse was scalded off me, chum.' But sure le next day, le phone was off le hook wih complaints. Broken sausages, squashed onion rings, soggy chips – Bananaman an Big Sally-Ann near gat le sack. But Big Sally-Ann pramised Nazi Nelly lat she woulden buck on le chippy's time no more, so we were allowed til stay on. Like Wee Bananaman musta been buckin on deliveries before, cos Sadie knew right away what had went on like.

Sure I coulden see Friday quick enough. I finally managed to get on til le till halfway through le week an was makin a wee fortune takin an extra quid off drunks an dickwads. But I didden nick off mammies or grannies or anybady like lat. Just spides, nob-heads an hoor-begs. I do have morals like.

Big Sally-Ann was still buckin Wee Bananaman in his delivery car. But lis time, ley did it on le front seat. Nie lem cars are a good size like. But hie thon big girl jockeyed up an down on him on le front seat I'll never know. I had visions of lem gettin stuck, mid-buck, an me havin til run round til le estate wih a tin opener til get lem out! But, at le end of le week, between our wages, Big Sally-Ann's tips an my nicked money, we had a few hundred quid between us. Here bes me, 'Frig, it'll nat get us far. All our food an drink an all's free isn't it?' Cos like I knew thon big girl cud ate ye outta house an home.

Here bes Big Sally-Ann, 'Awye. All we need is feg money – lat's it.' Le two of us had made appointments for crisis loans at le Bru, so we went down tilgether on le Friday afternoon. I was shit-scared of seein Mr Red White and Blue like. I'd seen him a couple of times since I last bucked him, but it was like dead awkward. He never spoke and neither did I. But he wasn't ler lat day. An Deirdre No-Diddies was nowhere til be seen either. I gat called in first. A wee twenty-year-old fella wih spots an nerd glasses it was. Here bes me, 'New here, chum?'

Here's him, 'Yes, I am.' Nen he smiled an I thinks til myself, he's smilin at le dolers, fuck me, he's gonna get ate alive in here, God love him. Anyhie, he went through le form super-quick. I telled him I needed two hundred quid til get a new cooker.

Here bes him, 'Did your old cooker break?'

Here's me, 'Awye, love. Too many Sunday roasts an all gettin cooked in it – it gave up.' Friggin only roast in my flat was le spit-roast I had wih lem two wee lawds from Short Strand. But yer wee man tuck it all in. Here bes him, 'Right – now I see you are still paying off a previous loan for … a sofa? Says here you got burgled and they took it?'

Here's me, 'Bloody right ley did.' But lat wasn't entirely true either. Big Sally-Ann an me gat tanked on Strawberry Cancorde one night an carried my sofa down til le boney til sit on while we smoked a few spliffs. Sure ya wanna seen le hack of it le next day, I had til leave it down ler. Ler was drink, sick an jiz all over it. Standard! Well, I saw on TV ler was a half-price sale on down in DFS endin lat night, so I run down til le Bru, dyin wih a hangover, gat le crisis loan an gat a taxi straight over til DFS. Gat ler wih ten minutes til spare til ley closed. Picked a leather one lis time, wipe-clean, paid le money an away I went, happy as Larry lat I'd made it for le end of le sale. Fuckin sale ended lat night, an started again at 8 a.m. le next friggin day. Conts.

Anyhie, my loan went through and so did Big Sally-Ann's. She said her aunt had died an she had til contribute til le funeral costs. Here's me, 'Frig, Sally-Ann lat's puttin a skud on yer aunt – what if somethin happens nie?' Like I'm a bit funny like lat. Ever since le time I walked under a ladder for a dare an gat knocked down by le lemonade man. Ack I wasn't hurt like, he was goin slow. But he give us free Cream Soda for about ten years after lat. So, I suppose it wasn't lat unlucky after all.

Here bes Big Sally-Ann, 'Ack, wind yer neck in.'

Her aunt was dead by dinnertime. Tuck a heart attack in bingo after gettin a full house. She woulda gat five hundred quid if she'd a shouted, 'House!' before she croaked it. But it wasn't til be. Big Sally-Ann's da was gutted like. Here's him, 'Fuck sake why didden she just shout "house" on le way down? Daft bat!'

We had til give him some of his money back til pay for le funeral – outta our crisis loans. Here bes me, 'I friggin told ya, Sally-Ann – it was a skud. Ya don't mess wih fate.'

Here bes her, 'Ack give over, she was about

25

ninety. She smoked fifty fegs a day an drank whiskey like tap water – I'm sure her liver was like a wrung-out shammie.'

So, we were back til a few hundred quid til spend on our halidays. But we had til make it do. We done our last shift on le Friday night in le chippy, an we were set to fly out to Benidorm on le Saturday. Nazi Nelly was ragin at us leavin her in le lurch. But I didden care. I coulden wait til get off le Road. I didden wanna see anybady – Nelly, Billy, Grotbegs – nobady. Big Sally-Ann said goodbye til Bananaman too. Here bes her, 'Ack, I was gettin fed up wih him til be hanast. He talks through his nose an he's a funny shaped schlong like.' Turned out wih all le shaggin in le front seat of his Mondeo, his dick had a permanent curve.

Here's me, 'Fuck! Bananaman! Lat's why he's called lat!' An Big Sally-Ann bust out laughin, here bes her, 'Fuck yer right, Maggie! Bananaman – beezer!'

Here bes me, 'I can't wait til get away from lese bendy-dicked, baby-makin fuckers an get a bidda Spanish sausage intil me!'

Here bes Big Sally-Ann, 'Ano, chum. A big

chorizo – spicy! Bring it on til fuck like!' So, we run up le Road yee-haain like two teenagers goin on ler first joyride.

4

Benidorm, here we cum ... literally!

Well, when we gat intil my flat, Big Sally-Ann an me started til tidy up. Nie, I only do lis twice a year – Christmas an le Twelfth. But goin on yer halidays kinda makes ya want til clean – even though ye'll nat be ler til enjoy it. I think I musta gat lat off Big Sally-Ann's ma. Sure she used til take us down til her caravan in Millisle in le summer when we were kids an le cleanin an washin lat went on le day before we went woulda put years on ye. Ler was windees washed, floors mapped, rugs shuck – le lat. Me an Big Sally-Ann even had til take all le VHS tapes out an make sure ley were all rewound. Like, luckin back, she was fuckin tapped! But le pramise of a go on le dodgems and a ninety-nine when we gat ler, was enough for us til sit an do it. So, lat must have like mentally scarred me an Big Sally-Ann cos we run about my flat cleanin like Kim an Aggie. No dish was left unwashed. An le ones lat had ground-in grease or hardened brown sauce on lem lat coulden be shifted went in le bin.

Ya wanna seen le stuff we found under le sofa an behind my TV unit. Big Sally-Ann's lucky Calvin Klein baxers, my George Best fiver an Big Sally-Ann's signed Peter Andre T-shirt lat she gat at his cancert last year. Sure we'd stud in le queue for near an hour til get them signed. But sure thon eejit wanted him til sign her diddies instead. Le luck on his face when she wallaped out le baps an shoved lem on his desk in front a him was pure beezer! Like, I think he was secretly delighted. Pity le security guard escorted her out. But I gat le T-shirts signed anyhie. An I gave him my buck-me eyes when he handed lem back til me. An he lucked at me funny an here's me, oh he'd get it. He'd get it BIG TIME! But sure, I gat ushered on out le door before I cud do anything else about it. Big Sally-Ann was sittin outside le shap cryin buckets. Le wee security guard was tellin her til calm down an she was shoutin, 'But I'm his friggin Mysterious Girl!' An le snatters were trippin her. Sure, I had til take her up til le Rangers Club an get her blacked – she was broken-hearted. Anyhie, she was all biz gettin her T-shirt back.

Here bes her, 'Oh frig, Maggie, we shud wear our Peter Andre T-shirts on le plane til Benidorm. It'll be amazeballs like!'

Here's me, 'Good idea, chum. Talkin of clothes, we shud get packed!' So, she run up home til shove a few outfits intil her case, an I did le same. Ya see, for feg runs ya have til pack light so lat ya have loads of space in yer case for le fegs yer gonna bring back. So, I shoved in a couple of my favourite outfits. My white bikini wih le shells on it, my leopard-print sarong, my gold stilettoes and two skin-tight dresses from Quiz, one see-through. Sure lat wud do me rightly. An anything else I needed, I cud get over ler. Sure le wee market at Benidorm was cracker for bargains. Well, I was just flingin my pink flip-flaps intil my case when wee Sinead

30

le greener rang. We hadn't seen much of her le last few months. She had met a wee fella from her road called Mickey an had been goin steady like. An Will an Sexy Anthony were goin strong too. We're talkin candlelit dinners, walks up le Cavehill hand in hand … le lat. We'd hardly seen lem two either.

Here bes her, 'Bout ye, big baps! What's happenin?'

Here bes me, 'Goin til friggin Benidorm le marra on a feg run, chum!'

Here's her, 'Jokin me! Benidorm? Friggin belter, chum!'

Nen she tells me lat Mickey'd came intil a bidda money an lat ley were luckin til go on haliday too. I wondered til myself when I'd see his bake up on *Crimewatch* like cos he's a skittery wee shite – ya coulden watch him like. Here's me, 'Why doncha come wih us? Get a late bookin – yez'll get it dead cheap an all!'

Here bes her, 'Nat a bad idea, chum – what hotel are yez in?'

Here bes me, 'No fuckin idea, chum – but it's near le bars an ley have free table tennis.'

Here bes her, 'Fuck me.'

Here bes me, 'Ano.'

Here bes her, 'Mickey an me'll go down til le wee travel agents here an see if we can get a flight – sure it'll be great craic if we can get tilgether. Wreck le fuckin place an all!'

Here's me, 'Awye, chum!'

Well, ley ended up gettin it booked. Same flights an all. Ley gat a hotel wih free table tennis, so we were sure it'd be le same one. Big Sally-Ann rung.

'Maggot – will I bring my denim knee boots or my silver platforms? Or both?'

Here bes me, 'Nie, Sally-Ann. Don't be packin loads – remember we've til fit thousands of fegs in our cases on le way back!'

Here's her, 'I'll go for le silver platforms len. Lem denim boots gives me a sweaty crotch anyhie.'

Here's me, 'Here Wee Sinead's goin an bringin Mickey!'

Here's her, 'Pure beezer – lis is gonna be some geg Maggie.'

Here's me, 'Ano. Nie hurry up. Get down wih yer case an all, an we'll have a few drinks before we hit le sack.'

Here's her, 'Awye will.'

Well. Ya wanna seen le case. Ya'd think she was emigratin til fuckin Benidorm.

Here's me, 'Whaaa?' Ler was skirts, dresses, tracksuits, a sombrero an her Deluxe Rampant Rabbit. Here's me, 'Are you right in le nut, chum? Some a lis stuff has gat til go. Startin wih le sombrero an le fuckin dildo!'

Here bes her, 'Ack I'll wear le sombrero on my head. An le dildo's gettin left ler cos I'm gettin a new one when I get back wih my prafits an all.'

Here's me, 'Why?'

Here's her, 'Saw a new one – le Thruster. I have my eye on lat.'

Here's me, 'Aye yer hairy eye.'

Here's her, 'Awye, chum. Ya know me too well.'

Here's me, 'Sure ya can get bucked twice a day in Benidorm if ya want til – ya don't need a dildo.'

Here's her, 'Ack, just in case like.' So, I shoved it back in again. Nen I lifted out lis battle a cream – like it lucked dead expensive. Here's me, 'What's lis?'

Here's her, 'A stole lat from le beauty salon le other day when I was in gettin my chin waxed.

It's anti-cellulite cream.'

Here's me, 'Whaaa?'

Here's her, 'I heard all le wee dolls talkin about it – ya put it on, len clingfilm yerself, an ya wake up le next day skinny!'

Here's me, 'Ack wise-ic Isaac, lem things don't work. Ley're for overpaid fuckwits wih money til burn.'

Here's her, 'Ack we may as well try it like. It cost us nathin. An I want rid of my orange-peel arse like.'

So, we plastered ourselves in le cream, nen we wrapped each other's bellies in le clingfilm. Big Sally-Ann clingfilmed her arse too. But len she needed a crap an had til take it off again. Eejit.

Well, we had til leave at four in le mornin til get to le airport. Sexy Anthony was pickin us up an all. We decided nat til get too blacked and til take it easy. Didden happen. Wee Sinead came down wih Mickey an brought a crate of Carlsberg Special.

Here bes Sinead, 'May as well just sit up all night an get pished, chum – no point goin til sleep!' So, we all ended up paralytic an when

34

Sexy Anthony came til pick us up, he near died. Here bes him, 'In the name a fuck, yez'll nat get on the plane in that state! Heck of yez!'

Nen he bundled us all intil le taxi, an away we went. Had til roll all le windees down like for fresh air – I was feelin a bit bokey. Here bes me, 'Lat Special did taste a bit rancid like – where did ya get it?'

Here bes Mickey, 'Round le back a Makro. In le skip.'

Here's me, 'Whaaa? Why were ley dumpin it? It musta been off!'

Here bes him, 'Nah. Ye'll be grand, love.' Well, I didden feel grand. I felt like my belly was doin le Mexican wave. An wih le cling film an all wrapped around it, well, I had le sweats like never before. We gat til le airport an I was glad of it. I bolted til le bogs and lashed rings round me. I coulda dug thon Mickey's face in for givin me rattan beer. But Big Sally-Ann an wee Sinead had stomachs of steel – didden even affect lem. Conts.

Well, we gat on le flight an Big Sally-Ann an me gat stuck beside some halfwit lat lucked like le Stay Puft mashmalla man from *Ghostbusters*.

I'm nat kiddin ya – he was massive. Le three of us were wedged intil le seats tilgether, an we literally coulden move le whole flight. I was in le middle. Big Sally-Ann fell asleep til le right a me, an le fat bastard fell asleep til le left a me. An I was stuck like Miss Piggy in le middle. Well, lat woulden a been too bad. Except yer man was fartin like a trooper from le Irish Sea til Gibraltar! I dunno what thon big lawd ate before he gat on le flight, but le smell of them farts reminded me of le time wee Dora Simmonds tried til gas herself in le flat beneath me. Sure her dog shit itself wih fright and le wafts comin outta thon flat woulda knacked ye out altogether. Dora made it like, but le auld dog Dusty slid on le shit, an fractured its skull on le hearth. It was an awful day. Anyhie, when we landed, I was near dead til get out for fresh air an a feg, so I bolted for le door.

'Meet yez at le baggage, ballbegs!' I guldered up le plane til my chums. Well. What a nightmare. After speed-smokin five fegs, I gat til le baggage, an Sinead an Mickey had ler bags on a trolley. An Big Sally-Ann was standin wih her face trippin her.

Here bes her, 'Maggot – our begs is lost! What are we gonna do nie?'

Here's me, 'Whaaa?' But she was right. Le begs were God knows where. In le end, we had til get on le coach an le wee rep said she'd chase lem up for us le next day.

Here's me, 'Oh Jaysus I need my lucky knickers, an my sexy dresses an all til touch!'

Here bes Big Sally-Ann, 'I swear on my granny's new hip, if we don't get lem begs back I'm gonna go boo-ga-loo!'

Here's me, 'Sally-Ann will you quit skuddin yer family like lat! Remember what happened til your aunt, fuck sake!'

Here bes Mickey, 'Ye'll never see lem again.' Nen he snuggled intil wee Sinead an here bes him, 'Fuck me, love, lis is le longest we've gone without buckin – it must be like twelve hours nie. My sac's like a beanbag.'

'Ano, love. Nat long nie,' says Sinead. An she petted his head like he was a wee pup. Here's me til myself, so lat's why we haven't seen her for months, she's been on a buckathon wih thon wee lawd.

Nen I snuggled intil Big Sally-Ann for sure I

was done in. A whole week a workin in le chippy an no sleep le night before an a hangover from hell. So, I closed my eyes an drifted off.

5

When in Spain, do as le Spanians do!

Well, I woke up about half an hour later til a bidda commotion. Sure we were at le first hotel stap an Big Sally-Ann was goin buck daft in le seat beside me.

Here bes her, 'Oh fuck, Maggot, please let lis be our hotel!' Nen I lucked over an Mickey was sittin wih his arms crossed, shakin his head. Here bes him, 'I am nat steppin fut in lat hotel.' Sinead was gigglin at him. So, I lucked out le windee an sure wasn't le hotel called Hotel Orange! Sure I near wet myself on le spat. Wee Sinead was windin Mickey up hummin le tune of 'Le Sash' an he was tuttin an all. But sure, it wasn't til be. Woulda been great craic like.

So, stap after stap, le names were called out an none a lem were ours. Here's me, 'Whaaa? Where in le name a fuck's lis hotel?' Well, ler was just us four an two people at le front left on le coach when we went down lis dirt track intil pitch black. Well, I thinks til myself, oh no, here we go again. Sure me an Big Sally-Ann had went til Kavos about ten years ago an ended up in a wee village in le arse-hole of nowhere. Sure ler was an auld donkey an all atein le grass outside le apartments. Sure it wasn't even apartments it was one-up, one-down wee shacks an we were le only tourists stayin ler. Went out til go til le beach one day (which was a two-mile walk) wih our lilos an *OK* magazines an le fuckin donkey was tatey bread! Some auld doll was dressed in black standin over it gernin. One a le wee kids lat lived in le village cud speak English an when we asked what happened til le donkey, she said a snake killed it! Fuckin Disturbia!

Well, about half a mile up le dirt track, le bus stapped. Nie, le hotel was gorgeous luckin. All modern an fancy, marble steps, le lat. But in le back of beyond. Le wee rep says it was le last stap – everybady off – so we all bounced off le bus, gaspin for a feg. Big Sally-Ann carried Sinead an Mickey's suitcases up til le reception while we stood outside puffin our brains out. Like it's a stressful time for smokers goin on haliday. Bein telled ya can't smoke for hours on end makes le cravin for a feg a matter of life or death til some people. Sure, at le airport I seen an auld man lightin up on le friggin runway, right beside le refuellin truck. Sure le wee Spanians workin in le airport went beserk, screamin for him til put it out in case le whole friggin plane exploded. But lat's le lengths people will go til. Like, it's no way til treat human beins like. By le time we gat intil le reception, lem other two from le bus had checked in, an it was our turn. Sinead an Mickey gat a room down le corridor from our room so lat was great. We all decided til drap our begs in an head down til le bar. Like all me an Big Sally-Ann had was our wee beach begs for hand luggage an in lem was make-up, fegs an magazines – so we coulden even go down til le pool for a swim nor nathin. Le room was pure beezer like. Ya get what ya pay for. Ler was a bathroom, tiled from floor til ceilin, a big mirra wih lights all around it. In le bedroom, ler was

41

a wee sofa an a lovely big bed wih loads a pillas an all round it. Pure luxury like. Nen I hears Big Sally-Ann in le bathroom, 'Here, Maggot – ler's two bogs in here. Is one for a pish and one for a shite or wha? Hie do ya flush lis thing?'

Here's me, 'Whaaa?' An I lucked in an sure she was sittin on le beeday wih her face screwed up. Here's me, 'Lat's for washin yer fanbax in, chum. In case ya drink le tap water an nen fally through – keeps yer arse tip-tap.'

Here bes her, 'Fuck me, Maggie, a fanny-washin machine? Pure beezer!'

Well, we hit le bar wih our tongues hangin out. We had wee red wristbands til prove we hadn't til pay for nathin. I ordered a vadki an orange an Big Sally-Ann gat a Sex-on-the-Beach cacktail. Here bes me, 'Ye'll be gettin one a lem for real le night, chum!'

Here bes her, 'Ano! We're gonna buck all round us lis haliday, chum!' An le wee barman drapped a wedge a lemon intil her glass an winked at her.

Here's her, 'Grassy hole, amigo!'

Here's me, 'It's nat grassy hole, ya plank - it's grassy arse.'

Here's her, 'Oh, awye.'

Nen here's me, 'He's a cert, chum.' An she winked back at him. Like Big Sally-Ann does pull le men on haliday like. Especially le foreign ones. Ler's just somethin about her lat lures lem in. Sinead an Mickey downed ler drinks an headed intil le pool. An by le way he trailed her in, I knew ley were gonna have an underwater ride within minutes.

Well, me an Big Sally-Ann were still in our Peter Andre T-shirts. An I was sweatin gravy like – so was Big Sally-Ann. So we tuck two sun loungers over til le back of le pool. Le beach was right behind us – it was like somethin outta *Wish You Were Here* like. We went under le shade of a wee bamboo umbrella an gat til gettin tanked on le free booze. Sure, we ordered lat many cacktails, in le end, le wee barman Juan filled two ice buckets up wih Sex-on-le-Beach an give us two straws. Sure it was amazeballs. Sinead an Mickey disappeared up til ler room til ate each other – sure ley coulden get buckin in peace in le pool cos ler was about ten auld lads swimmin round lem wih semis watchin. Ack ya coulden blame lem, Mickey was goin at Sinead's

43

nips like ley were dummy tits like. So it was just me an le big girl.

Well, wih no sleep le night before, ten ice buckets of Sex-on-le-Beach an le sound of le waves crashin against thon beach, le two of us fell asleep on le sun loungers. I woke up an it was pitch dark. Le pool was empty an le bar was closed. Here's me, 'Quick, Sally-Ann – wake up!' Sure she sat up an here bes her, 'Whaaa? What's happened? Where are we?'

Here bes me, 'It's fuckin midnight, chum – we've been asleep for hours!' So, we run back up til our room an sure, goin along le carridor, we heard wee Sinead an Mickey goin at it like le clappers. Ya wanna heard Mickey goin, 'Ugh, ugh, ugh, ugh!' Ya'd a thought he was liftin weights or somethin. So sure on le way past ler door, I shouts, 'Get it intil ye, yas dirty bastards!' An we hear wee Sinead shoutin back, 'Yeeeoowwwww!' She's pure dirt thon wee doll.

Well, me an Big Sally-Ann were boggin. Our Peter Andre T-shirts were stinkin a sweat – ler was no point gettin washed til put lem back on again. Here bes me, 'Mon we'll go out an get some clothes – sure le shaps is bound still til

44

be open.' So, we bounded out an run up thon dirt track like two gazelles. Well, le only shaps open was wee souvenir shaps. An all ley had was T-shirts sayin 'Kiss Me Quick' an all. I was in two minds whether or nat just til get one when Big Sally-Ann shrieks, 'Two of lese – lis is what we need!' Well, sure she had two Spanish señorita dresses in her arms – red-an-white wih spots an frills an all.

Here's her, 'When in Spain, do as le Spanians do!'

Here's me, 'Oh, go on len.' Wee bastard in le shap near robbed us frig sake, an I thinks til myself, we have til go easy on le money here like – we've fegs til get. Sure we had Nicotine Annie in le estate ready til pay us for our stash when we gat back. She was givin us a great wee deal like.

Well, we went back til le room til get changed. Le clingfilm round my belly was stuck fast. I near tuck a layer of skin away when I ripped it off me. I stood sideways in front of le mirra. An my belly lucked le same as before, only red from gettin squeezed til death all night. Here's me, robbin bastards – thank God we never paid

45

for lat cream. Big Sally-Ann was in le bogs, an I cud hear her squealin an laughin every couple a minutes. Here's me, 'For le sake lat is fuck – hurry up will ya? What are ya doin in ler anyhie?'

Here bes her, 'Fuck, Maggot, I'm gettin one a lese fanny-washin machines when I get home – beats le thruster any day!'

Iss is me til myself, Jaysus, thon big girl wud get off on a stiff breeze. Here's me, 'Mon til fuck, big girl – it'll be ler when ya get back!'

So, we linked arms, dressed til kill in our matchin señorita costumes, an marched down le carridor. We knacked on wee Sinead's door an she answered it in a thong. Her hair was a mess an her face was beetroot an she was breathless. Here bes me, 'Fuck sake, Sinead are yous still buckin?'

Here bes her, 'Ack awye, Maggie – go on without us. We haven't done it on le balcony yet an lat's Mickey's fantasy. Is it fancy dress le night in le hotel?'

Here bes me, 'No. No clothes remember? Sure we fell asleep at le pool an all le good shaps are shut.' Nen I hears Mickey callin her an here's me, 'His dick's gonna fall off, chum. Ye've been

46

at it for twelve hours nie!'

Here's her, 'Ano, ya wanna see it – ya'd think I'd give him a Chinese burn. We'll catch yous up sure.' Nen I hears Mickey shoutin from le balcony, 'Sinead, mon love, wee Mickey's ready for ya!' Nen she smiled an slammed le door.

Here bes me til Big Sally-Ann, 'Fair doos. Just me an you, chum – you up for it?'

Here bes her, 'Fuckin right, Maggot – mon da hell!' An we marched on down til le bar.

6

Grassy hole, amigo!

Well, it turned out ler had been a wee do on at le
bar an we'd just missed it. Sure we were ragin. Ler
was a Kim Wilde tribute act an a parrot on roller
skates. Sure it was one a'clack in le morning …
an le bar was closed. I coulda cried like. An Big
Sally-Ann was cryin. Aside from no drink, we
hadn't ate nathin since le day before, an I coulda
ate le leg off a baldy Russian. Len lis wee waiter
fella sauntered up til us wih a big smile on his
face an sure I near fainted. He was le double of
Peter Andre. Here bes him, 'Hello ladies, my
name is Sergio – you has arrived do-day?'

Here's me, 'Arrived? Arrived? I think I've
just arrived in my knickers, chum.' Nen he
lucks at me all confused an here bes him, 'I like

your dresses, señoritas. Le bar is clothed now – woulda you like somethink to dreenk? Sneaky, sneaky?'

Here bes Big Sally-Ann, 'Sneaky, sneaky – my legs are weaky. You luck like Peter Andre!'

Here bes him, 'Ah, yez, I heard that before. But I don't know this Peter Andre – is he good lookeen?' Nen he winked an I thinks til myself, I wonder hie many tourists he's bucked under le disguise of le Andre.

Here's me, 'He's all right. Nie whadda about sneaky-sneaky buck – I mean drink?'

An here bes him, 'Follow me.'

Well, me an Big Sally-Ann exchanged lucks at each other an she mouths til me, 'He's mine.' An I mouths back, 'No mine, yaconche.' But sure he tuck us downstairs intil le back of le restaurant. Sure it was like le staff quarters in *Dirty Dancin*. Ler was waiters, waitresses, security guards an chefs. Ley had all le dinner leftovers laid out in big silver trays, drink on tap, an a wee CD player playin Spanish music. Here's me, 'Whaaa?' Well, we gat stuck intil le drinks. It was rum an cokes an we'd never had lem before – sure ley only sell vadki in le Shebeen. But ley were gorgeous. Sure we were blacked in no time. Big Sally-Ann ate about fifty chicken drumsticks, an I gat wired intil le pizza. Big Sally-Ann was gettin birled round le place by Sergio Andre, while I was pourin us more drinks. Len I hears somebady say from behind me, 'Rum makes you come, señorita.' Well, I turned round an lucked intil his eyes an I poured le rum all over my own two feet. Sure standin in front a me was le actual double of Craig David. Nie don't snigger at me – I have loved Craig David ever since I seen him over at thon Odyssey at his wee cancert. Sure I ended up gettin a free ticket cos my cousin Linda's wee girl was a big fan an wanted til go. Sure ler was ten thousand kids … an len me. But he caught my eye when he was singin 'Fill Me In', an I'm tellin ya, my bush was agush. I was screamin, 'Fill ME in, yacontche!' It was a geg like.

Well, lis wee lawd was starin at me pourin le rum on my kebs an len he tuck le battle outta my hand an set it down. Here bes him, 'Are you okay, lady? You need to sit down? Some fresh air maybe?'

Here bes me, 'Fresh air, awye.' Sure I coulden wait til get thon big lawd outside. We walked down le steps til le beach, an he sat me down on a sunlounger. Here bes him, 'Travellink can make you feel strange – take in the air here. Breathe deeply.'

So, I breathed deeply, but even le noise of lat was settin my flaps on fire, so it was. Well, he sat down beside me an telled me lat he was le DJ at le hotel disco. An his name was Diego. Here's me, 'Whaa? Craig Diego?' An he laughs an here bes him, 'I don't know this Craig David – only English woman tells me every day I look like him. He must be very famous! You like him?'

Here's me, 'Like him? Well, I woulden kick him outta bed for fartin like!' Nen I stuck le lips on Diego. Like I near ate le wee fella. Nen when he came up for air, here bes me, 'Inter selecter – fill me in!'

Well, me an Craig Diego had a dirty ride down on le beach. It was le best first night of a haliday in le history of halidays. Even better lan le time me an Big Sally-Ann won le karaoke campatition in Butlins. Sure we done 'Jolene' by Dolly Parton an flashed our diddies at le end – gat a standin ovation an all. Won two free rides on le go-karts an a voucher for bingo. We were all biz.

But buckin a Craig David luckalike was like a dream come true for me. An like, after le shite few months lat I'd had, it was just le tanic I needed til get back til le good times again.

Big Sally-Ann ended up buckin Sergio, le Peter Andre luckalike, on le fish counter in le restaurant. Sure when I dandered back in wih Craig Diego, she was lyin on it wih her señorita dress up round her neck an Sergio Andre was atein prawns off her Mary. Craig Diego was skundered – he coulden get outta ler quick enough. He kissed my cheek an said he'd see me le marra. But Big Sally-Ann just gave me a thumbs up an shouts, 'Viva le Spanians!' Nen Sergio Andre mumbles from her crotch, 'Olé!'

Well, after Big Sally-Ann had finished and our boys had went til bed, me an Big Sally-Ann headed out til le pool wih two battles of rum. Sure we'd been asleep all day an we weren't for hittin le sack at all. It was le middle of le night an dead quiet – all we cud hear was le faint 'ugh, ugh, ugh' comin from high up. Here bes me, 'Lem two's still goin a dinger at each other up ler.'

Here bes Big Sally-Ann, 'Like I love a buck, Maggot, but lem two's nat wise.'

Here's me, 'Ano. Here, but what about Craig Diego an Sergio Andre – fuck me, chum we're buckin superstars!' An we high-fived each other.

Well, we downed le two battles of rum whilst discussin our boys' schlongs. Len Big Sally-Ann decides til go for a swim. Nie, here's me, 'Fuck sake, chum, we can't get our bras an all wet, sure we've none til change intil le marra.'

Nen here bes her, 'Maggot, we're in Asia. Get lem off!' Well, thon big girl whipped her kacks an all off, an she was as naked as le day she was born. Nen she jumps intil le pool. Here bes her, 'Oh, Maggot – it's amazeballs! I'm free, free as a bird!' So, here bes me til myself, fuck it – ya only live once. So, I tuck off me, an jumped in wih her. Well, we done le doggy-paddle, le breaststroke – an I mean le swim, I'm no lezzer – nen le backstroke. Sure it was pure beezer. Nen wih le yells an laughs an all of us, somebady musta heard us, cos I heard footsteps comin. Here's me, 'Duck!'

Here's her, 'Oh awye wih Hoi Sin sauce ... hhmmmm.'

53

Here's me, 'No! Duck!! Get down!' So under le water we went. But it was no good. We were snared a weeker. A big rough-luckin security guard came out til le pool an starts yellin an shoutin an all at us. Here bes me, 'Fuck sake, chum, we're only havin a geg like!' He was gulderin at us til get out! Get out! Well, I jumped out an wrapped a towel lat was lyin on a sunlounger round me. Nen le worst thing lat ya cud ever imagine happened. Le fuckin floodlights round le pool went on. Sure it was lit up like Ibrox Stadium for an Old Firm match. Big Sally-Ann was tryin til cover her diddies an stay afloat at le same time. Here bes her, 'I'm friggin naked – turn lem lights off!' But every time she shoved her baps under le water, ley floated back til le tap again.

Well, wih all le commotion, sure people started comin out til ler balconies an luckin down, an before ya knew it, ler was a hundred people glarin down at le pool wih Big Sally-Ann ballik naked in it. Well, sure she had til get out, so she run up le steps, bare arse in le air, an len she run behind a palm tree. Prablam was, le palm tree was about ten centimetres wide.

54

Sure all it hid was her belly button. One diddie either side an a big clump of fur down below. Ya wanna hear le gasps an le whispers comin from all le balconies. I lucked up an saw an auld lad grippin his chest like he was havin a cardiac an another one havin a sneaky ham-shank behind a deckchair. I near died for her like. Len I lucked up higher an I saw two pairs of chinos hangin over a balcony – an a fella peekin out from under lem. An it lucked like Mr Red White and Blue. But I coulden see in le dark, le rum had went til my head an was givin me hallucinations an all. So, I run over wih Big Sally-Ann's frock an she stuck it on – len we scarpered. Sure it was a pure shambles. We gat intil bed lat night an we were in stitches about it. Here bes Big Sally-Ann, 'Fuck I'm skundered. Le whole hotel's saw my fanny le night.'

Here bes me, 'Ano! Yer a friggin exhibitionist, chum! Get it intil ye like!' Nen she laughed an here's me, 'Don't worry, chum, it'll all be forgattan about le marra.' An we dozed off, still gigglin about le best first day of a haliday … like ever.

7

Hello Margaret

But it wasn't forgattan about. Le next day we rolled down til le restaurant for breakfast – well, it was really lunch, but breakfast til us. Wee Sinead had drapped off two sarongs for us cos sure we'd nathin til wear an no sign of our suitcases nor nathin. An Big Sally-Ann had tea-leafed two bikinis off le balcony next til us. Like mine was a tight fit round le diddies – but Big Sally-Ann's bikini barely covered her nips. It was like one a lem wee hats on a monks head. We walked down le middle of le restaurant, an all le waiters started clappin an cheerin an pointin at Big Sally-Ann an all. Sure le place was in an uproar.

Here bes me, 'Hie le fuck did all le waiters an all see ye last night? Sure ley were down here.' Nen one of lem points til le far wall. An sure wasn't it all glass. An what was on le other side? Le swimmin pool. Sure, me an her was swimmin up an down thon pool in le buff for ages. I was even givin le Muff a wee scrub while I was under le water an Big Sally-Ann was doin handstands an all. God knows what shapes lem wee waiters saw us in. Skunderation.

Here bes me til Big Sally-Ann, 'Play it cool.' So, I struts down le restaurant like I owned le place, an len I turns, swings my hand on to my hip an shouts out, 'Fanks. We're here all week.' Nen I tuck a bow. Well, le cheers of le waiters woulda deafened ya. It was like Paisley was down at le City Hall wih a 'No Surrender' banner.

An nen we gat stuck intil a pure feast of food. We're talkin steaks an chips, basketti bolognaise an Big Sally-Ann even gat wired intil a fuckin labster! Like, see lem all-inclusive halidays – ley were made for gluttonous bastards like me an Big Sally-Ann. Ya can pure stuff yerself wih food and drink le whole week – sure ya coulden bate it wih a big stick. I wanted til belly-slide along le dessert buffet bar wih my mouth agape like a baskin shark, swallyin le lat. Big Sally-Ann gat stuck intil her labster. Ya wanna see her tearin it til pieces. Legs ripped off, antlers picked out. Ya'd a thought she was doin an autopsy on it rather lan atein it. An I went back til le buffet for seconds. Sure ler was a wee man doin eggs, and ya cud have any kinda eggs ya wanted. Boiled, scrambled, poached, fried – le lat. So, I sauntered over an he asks me hie I'd like my eggs an here bes me, 'Unfertilised, chum.' Nen I busts out laughin but sure le joke was lost on le wee fella. He was all panicked-luckin, as if he was gonna get le sack for nat knowin hie til do unfertilised eggs. Here bes me, 'Two fried eggs, chum.' So, he flapped two on til my plate, an I turned round til go back to le table an sure who was behind me in le queue? Ya'll never guess. No, hanest – ya'd never get it in a million years. It was fuckin Mr Red White and Blue … an Deirdre-No-Diddies! Here's me whaaa? So, it was him jukein over le balcony at Big Sally-Ann's fanbax!

He was standin at le buffet wih his plate out an his mouth wide open an Deirdre was luckin me up an down over his shoulder. Well, here bes me, 'Oh a see. Didn't take you too long gettin back wih her. Bet ya were buckin her all along.'

Here bes him, 'Margaret. Please don't … Of course I wasn't …'

Nen Two-Backs pipes up, 'Come on, we don't have to listen to this.' So, I gets my plate wih le two fried eggs on it an shoves it under ler noses an says, 'Remind ya of anybady? Don't you be goin tapless or somebady'll be puttin you in a bap wih red sauce!' Nen I tramped off, tryin til keep my cool, but like inside I was friggin shakin like a shittin dog.

Well, when I gat back to le table, Big Sally-Ann was puttin what lucked like a labster's head intil her gob. She saw le luck on my face an here bes her, 'Ya can ate le head can't ya?'

Here bes me, 'Never mind lat – Mr Red White an fuckin Blue's over at le buffet wih friggin Deirdre-No-Diddies! Ley're here on haliday. Wih us. Oh Sally-Ann, lis is like my worst nightmare.'

Here bes her, 'Fuck me sideways – you're pure jokin me!'

Here bes me, 'No – luck.' An I points over.

Well, Deirdre-No-Diddies had an omelette on her plate le size of a wok an she was luckin over at me, snide like. Mr Red White and Blue was behind her, luckin at le floor. Here bes Big Sally-Ann, 'Til le beach – quick. We need til have a meetin about lis carry-on. I'll grab another labster an one a lem baguettes on le way out.'

So I gets up from le table, an here's me, 'Sure all le food is free – why do ya need til nick it?'

Here bes her, 'Ack, I fancy a snack after breakfast.'

Here bes me, 'Ya've just ate half le papulation of le Mediterranian Sea, chum.' But sure, she shoves a labster an two baguettes intil her beach bag on le way out le door. Well, I was all put about. I didden know what end of me was up. Big Sally-Ann trailed me down til le beach an we jumped on two sunbeds. Le wee waiter comes over til ask us what drinks we wanted an we both answer at le same time, 'Vadki on le racks!'

Here bes Big Sally-Ann, 'Nie Maggot, if ley think ley're gonna ruin yer haliday, ley've another thing comin. He's a no-good woman-batein bastard, remember? An she's a big drip.

Ya cud put holes in her back an use her as a flute, fuck's sake!'

Here bes me, 'Ano.' But til be hanast, I was rememberin him in lem chinos.

Nen she reads my mind an here bes her, 'An he'll nat be wearin chinos on haliday anyhie. Ya've nathin til worry about.' So, we stripped off til our bikinis an started downin le vadkis. An I thinks til myself, ack, she's right. I'm nat gonna let him ruin my haliday – I worked hard in le chippy for lis an I'm gonna friggin enjoy it. Len, I lucks over an Big Sally-Ann's flung her bikini tap off intil le sand.

Here bes her, 'Ack Maggie it's diggin intil my diddies somethin shackin. Sure nobady knows us here.'

Lis is me, 'Awye, suppose you're right.' Nen I flings my tap off too. Well, le wee barman came over til tap up our vadkis an Big Sally-Ann leaned over wih her plastic cup an near put his eye out wih her tit. Sure he was delighted! Here's him, 'Ladies, you must to put sun-cream on your skeen. Or you will go red … like lobster!'

Nen I says, 'Ack we'll be all right, chum. We lost our begs – haven't gat none – but sure we're used til le sun. We go til Dee's Sunbed Parlour on le Road all le time.'

Len Big Sally-Ann pipes up, 'Maggot I think we shud like evacuate here. Le men are off-le-scale rideable.'

Here's me, 'Awye … maybe.' Len, I settles down for a wee snooze. Nen I hears Big Sally-Ann say, 'Fuck a duck. Ler's Sinead an Mickey goin a dinger at it in le sea.' So, I lucks up an coulden see nathin. Nen I turns round an sure Big Sally-Ann has a pair a binoculars up til her eyes. Here's me, 'For le sake lat is fuck, what are ya at, woman?'

Nen she laughed, 'I brought lese til spy on le men … see who we're gonna pounce on après-ski.'

Here's me, 'Après-ski? We aren't fuckin skiing, chum!'

Nen she lucks all confused, 'I thought lat was Spanish for le night? My da was learnin me a few phrases before I left.'

Here's me, 'An what else did he learn ya?'

'Ahhh. Let me think. Oh … Izaborn aman – lat means, wud you like to dance, and what about ifaar tetyawan aschmellet? Lat means

62

you're pure gorgiz.'

I bust out laughin, 'Sally-Ann. Yer da's havin ye on, chum. Say lem phrases back til yerself slowly. Sometimes I wonder about you wee girl!'

Well, I tutted an tuck le binoculars off her an started til luck around le beach while she was mumblin til herself an cursin her da. Sinead an Mickey were goin for it right enough. Ler was a crowd a English wee lads all drinkin beer an laughin, an I wondered if ley were stayin at our hotel. Like Craig Diego was amazeballs, like, but ler's nathin bates an English sausage. Nen I scans along le shore an stapped dead. Sure ler ley were. Hand in hand. Mr Red White and Blue an Deirdre-No-Diddies walkin along le beach, kickin le waves lat crashed til le shore. An every kick was like a stab til my heart. Big Sally-Ann had fell asleep cos ya cud hear le snores of her from Portugal. So, I downed my vadki, len I downed Big Sally-Ann's, an I spent le rest of le afternoon watchin Mr Red White and Blue and Deirdre-No-Diddies actin like ley were in a shit eighties love story. I was ragin when she kissed him in le water, an I was near gernin when he was rubbin suncream intil her back. Or it may have been her front – it was hard til tell.

Watchin le carry-on of le two of lem, I felt like Big Sally-Ann's labster lat was festerin in her beachbeg. Rattan, forgattan an stinkin somethin shackin.

8

Sticky Vicky skunders Mickey

Well, after a couple of hours of pure torture, Mr Red White and Blue an Deirdre-No-Diddies started til pack up. I put my binoculars down an rolled on to my front so ley coulden see my face as ley went past. But I still heard Two-Backs gigglin an him mumblin somethin til her an sure I wanted til bury my head in le sand so I didden have til listen. I knew ley were goin back til le hotel room til buck. After ley were gone, I rolled back over, closed my eyes tight so lat no tears cud escape, an fell asleep.

Well, I had a dream lat Mr Red White and Blue had me tied til le bed. I was lyin on my back like a starfish, ballik naked. He was on his knees between my legs an he had lat wee half-smile lat I hadn't seen in months. Sure I was moist, so I was. Nen he brings out a big torch thingy wih fire on tap, like le Olympic flame. An sure before I cud say, 'Stap, don't!' he run it down le front of my bady, burnin me. I was scalded, screamin and strugglin til get outta le bed. Well, I woke up on le beach wih a crowd round me. I was lyin on le sunbed on my back, tapless. Here's me, 'Whaaa?' Nen lis auld doll points at my diddies an heres her, 'Love, you're sunburned really bad – you'll need to get something on that to calm it down.' Nen she points at Big Sally-Ann, 'And your friend's the same there.' Well, I lucked over at Big Sally-Ann. Sure she was lyin on le sunbed uncanscious, wih her mouth wide open, an le slabbers were trippin her. An she was bright red, from le tap of her forehead, right down til her ankles. Luckily for her, her diddies had slid til le side an were near under her arms – so it was only her cleavage lat was beetroot. I wasn't so lucky. My baps were red raw, like two balls of corned beef, and my nips were like raisins an burnt til a crisp. So, I jumps up an yells, 'Chum – we're scalded!'

Nen Big Sally-Ann jumps up an here's her, 'Whaa, whaa?' Nen she sits up an her diddies swing back intil position, an as soon as ley touch her belly again, she lets a scream outta her lat wud break glass. Here's me, 'Quick – til le restaurant. We need til plaster our baps in somethin cold!' So, we grabs our stuff an runs through le hotel screamin. Well, we gat til le restaurant an sure Craig Diego was standin at le door. Here bes him, 'Ladies the restaurant issa clothed. Come later ... seex o'clock.'

Here bes me, 'Let me in there nie! We need some yoghurt til cool us down.' Len I opened my sarong til show him my crusty baps an he gasped an let us in. So, God love him, he went intil le kitchen til get us some an when he came back, I'd leaned my baps intil a bucket a ice, an Big Sally-Ann had dropped her diddies intil a basin of chocolate ice cream. We grabbed le yoghurts an scarpered back til le room. Well, I'm tellin ya – le pain was like nathin else. Worse than le time I caught my diddie in le fridge door when I was buckin Big Billy in le kitchen. An definately worse lan le wallapin I got off Mr Red White and Blue.

Big Sally-Ann was lyin on le bed, plastered from head til toe in apricot yoghurt before ya cud say Müllerlight. Len she let a big sigh out of her. Here's me, 'Whaaa?'

Here bes her, 'Yoghurt on sunburn's as satisfyin as a Sunday mornin shite, chum.'

Here's me, 'Awye.' So, we lay on le bed for ages talkin about our boys and ler chorizo sausages an all. Len we hear a knack at le door. Big Sally-Ann answered it an it was wee Sinead an Mickey. Well, Mickey tuck one luck at us wih our baps out an here's him, 'I'll wait outside, love, lem two's nat wise.' Well, Sinead told us she was pure knackered wih all le shaggin and she wanted us all til have a big night out – like a change of scenery an all. Pure bender. She went an gat us some aloe vera til put on our baps an we shoved our Spanish dresses on again an away we went.

Down at le wee hotel bar, ler was another do on. Ler was a magician lat was tryin til cut one of le waiters in half, Spanish dancers wih clapper thingies in ler hands, an drink on tap. I felt all cultured an all. Me an Big Sally-Ann gat a jug of sangria. Sure it was pure beezer – it had fruit an all floatin in it. Nie it was a bit tarty at le start, but once it burned le taste buds off your tongue, it wasn't too bad. Craig Diego was behind le DJ bax an he winked over at me, an I winked back. Here bes Wee Sinead, 'Check out yer man le DJ! Here isn't he le double of …'

Here's me, 'Craig David … ano. Bucks like him too.'

Here's her, 'Whaaa?'

Here's me, 'Oh awye. Nailed him on le beach le first night, chum. You've missed loads lacked in lat room wih Mickey le sex machine.'

Here's her, 'I haven't half – check out Big Sally-Ann!' Nen I lucked over til le bar an sure she had Sergio Andre up against it an she was givin him a tug through his trousers.

Here's me, 'Awye – he's le Peter Andre one. Ley're everywhere, chum.'

Nen here's her, 'Fuck I shoulda left Mickey at home an gat myself one a lese wee lawds. Fuckin ragin nie.'

Well, after a couple of hours of sangria, an a few twirls round le dancefloor, we decided til go out on le town. I told Craig Diego we'd meet up down at le staff do later on lat night an off we went. Sinead an Mickey hadn't even left le hotel grounds up til len – an ley coulden believe our hotel was so far from le town. When we gat til le town, we were all dyin for a drink.

First stap was a wee Irish bar called Shenanigans – Sinead an Mickey were up dancin from le word go til all le wee republican songs. Like me an Big Sally-Ann were a bit put out, bein from le Road an all. Wee Sinead tried til get us up dancin an here's me, 'Naaah, chum – get lem til play "le Billy Boys" an I'll be skippin up til thon dance floor, chum!' Me an Big Sally-Ann were more interested in le 'buy one shat get ten free' offer. Sure ley tasted like Ribena – we were downin lem one after le other. After about half an hour, we were ravin til le wee rebel songs, an didden give a shite who knew it! Was a pure geg. Nen we went on til le next bar. An sure who was just startin ler show? Sticky Vicky. What a woman! Sure I remember le first time I went til Benidorm – I was about twenty an she was about sixty. So what fuckin age was thon auld doll nie? She must be a hunderd. Wee Sinead an Mickey hadn't a baldy who she was, so I telled lem lat she was a magician. Well, she kinda is like! Makes things disappear an all!

Well, Big Sally-Ann gat a ringside seat –
literally. Sure she loves a bidda Sticky Vicky. She
tried til copy her one year when we gat home
til impress wee Eggy Moore, an ended up in le
Mater wih a Linfield scarf stuck up her clout.
Eejit. Mickey came til le table wih drinks for us
all. He was blacked. Here bes him, 'Ladieeze,
lese are called Slingapore Sings – get em intil
yeez.'

Here's me, 'Whaaa?' But len, le show started.
Well. Ya wanna seen Sinead an Mickey's faces.
Pure picture. Sticky Vicky gat a big pencil, like
a stick of rack, an sharpened it wih her glory-
hole. Len, she bent down, an pulled all le flegs of
le world out in a big string. Here bes Big Sally-
Ann, 'I wonder has she le one from le City Hall
in her blirt!' Mickey was amazed. Here bes him,
'Hie does she do it? Like hie? Hie?'

Nen here bes Sinead, 'Here don't you be
gettin any idears, wee lawd. My Mary's red raw
already – without le hide-le-furniture game.'

Well, le finale was pure beezer. Sticky Vicky
gat a battle a beer, came right up til Mickey an
flung one leg up on le chair he was sittin on.

71

Sure he didden know where til luck. Nen she tuck le battle, stuck it up her muff, an out it came wih le tap off. Nen she give it til Mickey an he tuck a swig. Here bes him, 'Boke. Must be le local stuff – nat nice.' An le place went intil an uproar. Sure she gat a standin ovation. An lat was sayin somethin because hardly anybady cud even stand.

Well, after lat, we were lat steamin, we decided til head back til le hotel. We coulda stayed an chased le men in le bars like. But we were sweatin buckets in our Spanish dresses an sure we had Craig Diego an Sergio Andre waitin til ride us intil le wee hours. Wee Sinead an Mickey wanted til get back an buck on le beach so we all left tilgether. I winked at Big Sally-Ann, here's me, 'See, chum – lis haliday's turnin out til be pure amazeballs like.'

Here's her, 'Ano.' Nen she lifted le battle a beer lat Mickey had set down an downed le lat in one go.

9

A lumber in le moonlight, an a burnt hand til boot

Well, on le way back up le dirt track til our hotel, Big Sally-Ann needed a slash. An thon big girl can't hold it in – when she has til go she has til go. She's like a six-futt taddler. So, Wee Sinead an Mickey power-walked back til le hotel, cos Mickey was gaggin for it, an we went til squat in le bushes. Sure I coulden watch somebady else pishin without pishin myself. It's like contagious til me. So, we stepped off le dirt track, hoisted up le ruffles on our dresses, took our kacks down an opened le floodgates. Sure it was pitch black – ya coulden see a thing. Nen, I feels myself slippin a bit an here's me, 'Sally-Ann I hope yer nat pishin in my direction, chum! I've only one friggin dress remember!' It's nat le first time she's splashed me like. Sure she can pish up a wall if she wants til – her fanny's like a water cannon on tap of a meat wagon in le Ardoyne riots.

But here's her, 'No, chum. I'm nat, I'm aimin at le ground … it's all slippy where I am too.'

Here's me, 'Whaaa? What are we pishin on? Is it leaves or whaaa?' But sure we coulden see nathin under us at all it was lat dark. So, we trailed ourselves up an headed back til meet our boys.

Well. Le staff do was in full swing. Luckily for us, ler was more men lan women, an nobady had tried til nick our boys. Craig Diego was sittin on a chair beside le door smokin a feg. Le moonlight was shinin in through le glass door lightin him up in le darkness. Sure he was pure gorgeous. I was drippin. I sauntered over an here bes me til him, 'Bout ya, hat racks.' Nen he pulls me on til his knee an sings intil my ear, 'I wanna kiss you all over … and over again … boom boom boom … when the night closes in.' Nen he goes all high-pitched an sings, 'When the night closes in.' Well, I thinks til myself, nobady has ever sung til me before … sure it was like le

74

Irish Sea down ler … an le tide was out! Here bes me, 'You'll do me, chum! Nie where do ya want me?'

Nen he tells me lat he wants til ride me in le sand under le moonlight. Here's me til myself, nie ya don't get an offer like lat in le Shebeen on a Saturday night! Sure I was all biz. I tuck his hand an glanced over at Big Sally-Ann. She was sittin wih Sergio Andre an on le table between them was a cucumber, a banana, a courgette an a fuckin butternut squash! She lucked like she was askin him til pick one. Here's me, ah frig she's gonna do a Sticky Vicky again. But sure when yer on yer halidays, ya just go wih le flow.

Well, when I gat out til le beach, le only light was le moonlight. Le black sea had a sparklin stripe down it where le moon was reflected. It was pure gorgeous. For a split second I wondered if Mr Red White and Blue had seen le moon like lat. Nen I pushed le thought of him til le back of my mind.

Here bes Craig Diego, 'What is wrong, lady? You are not happeee? Look I have made nice place for us.' Nen I lucked behind me an le wee lawd had wee lit candles in le sand in le shape of a heart. Ler was a battle a fizzy wine an two glasses sittin on a sunlounger an all. Here's me, 'Whaaa? Do you do lis for all le tourists ya buck like? Must cost ya a fortune in candles!'

Nen he laughs an here's him, 'You are funny lady. Eees why I like you – you speak mind an are not afraid. Not like normal girls. They want love and marriage – you just want fun and penis.'

Here's me, 'Awye. That's me. Just fun. Not normal.' An I laughed an lifted le battle of fizzy wine and tuck a few glugs. Nen I thinks til myself, am I nat normal? Lis wee lawd's known me two days an he knows already lat I'm nat a keeper. An I dunno if it was le drink or nat but I felt a bit teary. Nen I seen movement til le right of me, an Craig Diego seen it too. Here bes him, 'Ah. We havth company on the beach! Let's wait. I go get us some food before we do the sex, yes?'

Here bes me, 'Awye will.' So, he dandered off an I sat an lucked at le moon on my own. I didden feel lat drunk anymore, just fuzzy an tired. An my Walter Mittys were startin til burn again. I pulled my dress out at le neck an tuck a luck down at lem an says, 'Yip. Still beetroot.' Nen I

76

hears more movement an sees a head poppin up.

'Margaret? Is that you?' Well, I was about til bolt but when I put my hand down til hoist myself up, I put it on a fuckin candle an burnt le hand off myself. Sure I screamed le place down. Nen I jumped up but it was too late. He saw me.

'Margaret, Margaret – wait.' It was Mr Red White and Blue.

'Luck. What is it? If you're buckin Two-Backs down ler, I don't wanna know, okay?'

'No, Margaret. I'm alone.' Nen he was standin in front of me. He had a white linen shirt on lat was open til halfway down his six-pack. An a pair a fuckin chinos. Bare futt. Here's me, great.

Here's him, 'Are you okay? Have you burnt your hand? Let me see.' Nen he lifts my hand an sure le minute he touched me, I just wanted til ate him, nob first. He was luckin at my hand in deep cancentration unaware lat le Muff was veerin towards him like a magnet.

Here's me, 'What are ya doin down here on yer own?'

Nen he lucked up at le sky, 'Just looking at the moon – it's beautiful, isn't it?'

I shrugged, 'S'all right.'

Here's him, 'I was thinking of you, Margaret.' Well, me an my groins cud take no more. I lumbered le bake off le bastard. We were like animals. I grabbed le back of his neck, an he pulled me in by le waist, we were breathless. Len I hears, 'Ahem, ahem'. Mr Red White and Blue stapped kissin me an I twirls round an sure Craig Diego was standin ler wih a big silver tray wih chicken drumsticks an sandwiches an other bits an bobs on it. Mr Red White and Blue steps back an says, 'Sorry, I'm sorry. I didn't realise. I must go because … Deirdre.' Nen he starts til run off.

Here's me, 'Wait…' But he was gone.

Craig Diego sits down wih le platter a food an doesn't luck like he gives a shit lat I was just lumberin le bake off somebady else. Here's him, 'Sit, sexy lady – eat.'

I tuck a drumstick off him, 'Lat was my ex-boyfriend. He's here wih his new girl. She's gat no diddies. Like two pancakes – ye've prabably seen her about. Bowl haircut?' Craig Diego shook his head.

Here's me, 'Lotta history ler. Didn't end too well.'

Nen he put his arm round me, 'You want him

back? You love him?'

I laughed, 'Naaaaaa. Course nat! He's a bastard!' Nen Craig Diego smiles an offers me a sandwich. I tuck it an flung it over my shoulder. Nen I pure molested le wee lawd. Le two of us rolled about in le sand lat much, we were plastered in le stuff. Sure his balls was like two Skatch eggs. But, every time I closed my eyes, I was imaginin bein ler wih Mr Red White and Blue instead of Craig Diego. Like he was gorgeous – an any other time I'd have been delighted til be buckin a Craig David luckalike. But there was just somethin about Mr Red White and Blue … a connection. I coulden get him outta my mind. It was like unfinished business. Ya know like if ya cut yourself an it scabs … an ya know nat til touch it and ya tell yourself nat til touch it, but ya can't rest til ya pick it? Well, lat was what it was like wih Mr Red White and Blue.

After me an Craig Diego were done, we dandered back til le restaurant. Big Sally-Ann an Sergio Andre were nowhere til be seen. So, I headed back til le room, gat intil bed an dreamt of Mr Red White and Blue kissin me in le moonlight.

10

A kumquat in yer twat

Well. Le next mornin, I woke up til le door near gettin put in. I heard le faint sound of Big Sally-Ann's voice shoutin, 'Maggot, Maggot! Let me in!' So I runs til le door an opened it. Well, she bounced in wih her eyes standin on her head.

Here bes me, 'What time is it?'

Here bes her, 'Six a'clack, chum.'

Heres me, 'Whaaa? Where have ya been all lis time like?'

Here bes her, 'Oh Maggot, it was a nightmare, chum. I ended up in le Benidorm Medical Centre!'

Here's me, 'Frig me, what for? Are ya all right like?' Nen she sits down an lights a feg for both of us. Here's me, oh here, lis must be good. Nen

80

she starts til tell me about her puttin on a wee Sticky Vicky tribute show for Big Sergio Andre.

Here bes me, 'I knew it! I friggin knew it when I seen all lem vegetables on le table last night!'

Here bes her, 'Sure didden I call myself "Slip 'n' Slide Sally-Ann" like. It all went okay at le start – I was qware an good at it like! Big Sergio was lovin it – le cucumber, le salami, le butternut squash … but len I run outta veg, chum. An I wanted til end it on a big finale thing.'

Here's me, 'Don't tell me ya shoved a battle a Buckey up yer quim?'

Here's her, 'No! Don't be daft – sure ley don't sell lat here.'

Here's me, 'Awye, right enough.'

Here's her, 'Sure le only thing I cud get my hands on was a couple a lem wee yella things like big grapes – ya know, lat ya get shoved on le side of le cacktail glasses?'

Here's me, 'Whaaa? Kumquats?'

Here's her, 'Awye! Lem! Sure I was rememberin what ya telled me about lem silver balls ya gat one time in Ann Summers.'

Here's me, 'Frig I forgat about lat!' Sure

81

didden I send Big Billy Scriven down til Ann Summers for a twenty quid mix-up one time after he gat his claim for goin over on his ankle on a broke grate. An he came back wih silver balls an a blow-up doll. Big gallute! I says til him, 'Billy … are you nat right in le head? What in le name a fuck am I gonna do wih a blow-up doll?' But he says he always wanted til have a threesome, but coulden bare til share me wih a real person. Here's me til myself, 'Ack.' Nen I wallaped him round le head wih it. Ended up sellin it til Thelma le hermaphrodite for a fiver up at le Shebeen one night. God knows what happened til it after lat! Sure Big Thelma left early – even before le ballot was drew for le ten-glass battle a Vadki! Anyhie, me an Billy had a go wih le silver balls. Nie it wasn't my cuppa tea. Sure I hadn't a baldy notion what til do wih lem – ley were in an out like le dusty bluebells fuck sake! But Big Sally-Ann thought ley were amazeballs … literally. So lat's why she had a go wih le kumquats. Fair play til her like.

Here bes her, 'Frig, I rammed a few of lem in, an len tried til shoot lem out at Big Sergio Andre. But ley woulden come out. It was awful.

82

We tried everything – tweezers, a skewer from le barbeque, a meat hook … an nathin. Sergio even gat le industrial hoover from le cleaners' store an had a go wih lat – but ley weren't for budgin.'

Here's me, 'Whaaa? Are you tellin me ya ended up in hospital wih a bunch a kumquats stuck in yer twat?'

Here's her, 'Awye. Skundered.'

Here's me, 'Skundered all right, chum! I'm sure yer fanny's in tatters.'

Here's her, 'Ack, it's all right. An le wee dacter says lis happens all le time here. All le Sticky Vicky wannabes gettin ler fanbaxes cleared out. He said le best one was a woman from Hull wih one a lem musical merry-go-round ornaments lodged in her drainage. Sure everytime she sneezed, her fanny sung 'Yankee Doodle Dandy'!

Seriously but. Thon Sticky Vicky must have a fanny le size a Royal Avenue. Like she's some talent.

Anyhie, after Big Sally-Ann had a go on le beeday, we decided til go down for breakfast early like. Sure we never made it for breakfast on any of our halidays – unless we were only comin in from an all-nighter or somethin – but len we were too pished or wiped out til remember what it was like. So, we headed down til le buffet an I started til tell Big Sally-Ann all about my night – meetin Mr Red White and Blue an all. Like, I knew what her reaction wud be.

'Oh, Maggot! Don't! He's a badden – remember what he did till ya le last time?'

Here's me, 'Awye … ano. But, he seems different nie. Like all calm an all. He was out on le beach on his own, luckin at le moon an all like.'

Nen she laughed, 'He shud be on le fuckin moon, chum. Pure spacer him.'

I lucked at my feet, 'Ack, people change, chum.'

Nen she tuck a bite of her Spanish omelette an said, 'Don't you be actin a maggot, Maggot. Listen. A tiger never changes his spats. Think about lat.' Nen somethin catches her eye an she draps her fork an here's her, 'Luck! Ley've just put out whole chickens! For breakfast! Can ya imagine? Chickens for breakfast! I'm away til get one – ya want one too?'

I nodded, 'Awye will, may as well. Get us a

well-done one. Line our stomachs for a day of drinkin, chum! Job's a gooden!' So Big Sally-Ann skipped off til le buffet an I poured myself another cuppa coffee. An I was just decidin whether til have a cheesecake or a profit-roll tower for breakfast dessert when I hears a wee voice say, 'Excuse me, love, can I borrow your milk?' Nen I turned round an ler was a wee girl an fella sittin at le table behind me. Here's me, 'Ack awye, love, certainly. Keep it – sure I don't want it back!'

Lis is her, 'Awye – right enough!' Nen I realises she's a wee Belfaster – just like us! Here's me, 'Ack chum, I didden realise you were from wee Norn Iron! So are we!' Like ler's nathin as satisfyin as hearin a wee Belfast accent amongst all le softly-spoken English an le machine-gun-speakin Spanians.

Here's her, 'Ack yes. We saw yous on le bus, like, on le way here. We got off first. S'lovely hotel isn't it? Free table tennis an all! Have ya seen le waiters? Aren't they big rides?'

Nen we laughed an here's me, 'I've seen lem all right, chum!' An I wondered whether or nat till tell her I was buckin one a lem. Nen her fella pipes up, here's him, 'Here, you! You're spoken for!' Nen we all laughs. Nen Big Craig Diego slides up til me an here's him, 'You like a fresh percolator, lady?'

Here's me, 'Haa-whaaa?'

Here's him, 'A coffee percolator?' Nen he points at le pat in his hand.

Here's me, 'Ack! Is lat hie ya say it in Spanish? We say 'teapat' in English, chum.'

He lucked all confused, 'But percolator is English word … Also, it is not tea, it is a coffee. You for coffee?'

Here bes me, 'Naaa. You fo-coffee. Go on you fo-coffee, ya conche!' Nen I slapped his arse as he tratted off til le next table. Len le wee girl behind me giggles an here's her, 'Oh you're a pure geg, love! You fo-coffee! Beezer!' Nen Big Sally-Ann sat down wih two whole chickens an half a chocolate gateau, Sinead and Mickey came to join us an we all had a great wee chinwag. Le two were called Dean an Dawn, from Rathcoole, like, an ley were great craic. Here bes Dawn, 'We found a wee beach – it's a bidda a trek like but ler's no kids nor nathin. Pure paradise! Yez wanna come wih us today?'

Here's me, 'Whaaa? Yer jokin me! Brill!' Sure I was getting fed up a sittin like scalded sardines down on thon beach. Le day before some wee girl had started a water fight wih Big Sally-Ann, so I ducked her in le sea an she started gernin an all. Her ma was givin me dirty lucks le rest of la day like. Well, don't start what ya can't finish – lat's what I always say, whether yer a ten-year-old or nat.

So, we horsed our breakfast intil us an went til get ready for our trip til le private beach. Big Sally-Ann swiped a battle a rum on le way out of le restaurant an I nicked a battle a pink fizzy wine too – so we were sorted. Here's me til myself, le day's gonna be a geg. Great craic wih some quality chums, an a pure-fire distraction from one ridey hornball called Mr Red White and Blue.

11

Dean an Dawn – le Rathcoole nudists

Well. Me an Big Sally-Ann were first down til reception. We asked cud we see le rep til ask if our begs had turned up yet but ley said Reuben woulden be ler til dinnertime. So we said we'd be back len. Like I was spittin bricks, like, lat ley hadn't turned up. I was dyin til get my wee halterneck mini-dress on til impress le fellas – an a change of knickers at least. We'd our beach begs full of drink an fegs an all. We had til go intil le wee supermarket beside le hotel an get suncream cos of our scorched diddies. Sure I was payin for it at le till when le big girl runs up til me like a pure child wih two big plastic things – one blue an one green. Here's me, 'What's thon?'

Here bes her, 'Oh Maggot – we have til get lese for le beach, it'll be a pure geg. Blow-up whale an a blow-up cracadile!'

Here's me, 'We've still til buy le fegs, ya tool – we're gonna have no money left like.' But she was doin lat pleadin thing she does wih her eyes – like one a lem hush puppy dogs, so I says, 'Oh, all right will. But we're goin til buy le fegs le marra all right? No more money's getting wasted.' Sure she was all biz like, an I had til smile.

Well, Dean an Dawn sauntered down wih towels under ler arms an nen Sinead an Mickey came down too, an we all set off for le private beach. But here, on le way down le wee dirt track, I near died. We were just passin le spat where me an Big Sally-Ann had pished le night before an sure ler was about a hundred wee frogs all jumpin about what lucked like a swamp. Here's me, 'Whaaa?' til Big Sally-Ann an here's her, 'Oh Maggot, we musta been slippin an slidin an pishin on all lem frogs in le middle of le night. Boke like.'

Here's me, 'Ano, chum – I squatted on fuckin Kermit's bake. Head melter!'

Nen here bes her, 'Awye, ya never saw lat on le Muppets, chum!'

Anyhie, we sauntered on down til le beach. Sure Dean an Dawn were stormin ahead an Sinead an Mickey were already touchin each other up, seein as ley hadn't bucked in like an hour-an-a-half, an me an Big Sally-Ann were trailin behind. It seemed like miles we'd walked, an we were goin way out of le town. I was sweatin buckets an I was about til do a wee sit-down protest when Dawn shouts back, 'Just down this wee track here, an we're there!' So, we hurried on an caught up wih lem. Well, as we went down le wee dirt track, I heard le sounds of le sea, waves crashin an all, an I coulden wait til go an have a dip, len get wired intil le drink. An when we gat to le bottom of le track, we went round a wee hedge an ler it was. Le private beach. Just a few people dotted around le place on towels, some in le sea, an a few playin bat an ball at le shore … an no kids.

Here's me til Big Sally-Ann, 'Nie, lis is what I call a beach, chum.' Nen I winked at Dawn an she winked back len giggled. An I thinks til myself, ack, she's a lovely wee girl like, sound as a pound. Len I wallaped off my Peter Andre T-shirt, an I cursed le wee bikini tap lat we'd nicked. Sure my diddies were pure squashed intil it an it was cuttin off le blood supply. So, I lucked round an Big Sally-Ann was havin le same problem. Nen, I lucked over at Sinead, an she'd tuck Mickey by le hand, an run down towards le sea for a quickie. Nen, I lucked at Dean an he winked at me, nen he whacked off his shorts, an he was ballik-naked underneath. Here's me, 'Whaaa?' Sure, I thought he'd pulled his baxers off along wih lem by mistake – so I lucked le other way like. But when I lucked at Dawn, sure she was ballik-naked too! I turned round til glare at Big Sally-Ann, but she was fixed on Dawn's boobs. Here bes her, 'Dawn, is lem baps fake like?'

Here bes Dawn, 'Oh, no! All real – 100 per cent.' Nen Dawn grabs her baps an gives lem a squeeze. Well, if ya'd have seen Big Sally-Ann's face. She didden know where til luck. Nen I lucked a bit closer til le people lyin down on le towels like, an nen I realises … lis was a private beach all right – a fuckin nudists' beach!

Nie, I'm no prude. Sure I flashed my diddies til five thousand people when Linfield won le cup at le Oval lat time. An sure I tried til get on til le *Embarrassin Bodies* program on le TV lat time. Sure le wee van was down le town in Cornmarket wih le lovely Dr Christian standin ler, luckin for valunteers like. So I gat in, whipped my kacks off an showed him le mole lat I have on my fanbax. Cos sure I'd been goin on le sunbed ballik naked an wanted it checked. Ya can't be too careful wih lem UDA rays like. But sure he near died. Turned out he was ler til film *Supersize versus Superskinny* an was wantin til ask me about hie often I exercised! An all he gat was a face fulla flange! Geg like. So, I wasn't shy about gettin le Muff out ... nie an again. But runnin about a beach buck-naked was nat somethin lat I thought I'd ever do. So I kept my bikini on.

Big Sally-Ann was strugglin til tuck her chebs intil her bikini tap, nen she turned round til me an here bes her, 'Think I'd be all right goin tapless here, Maggot? Feel wick in fronta Mickey an all like.'

Here's me, 'Chum. Luck around ye.'

Here's her, 'Why?'

Here's me, 'Just luck.' So, she sits down on her towel beside me an squints her eyes. Nen here's her, 'Fuck! Ler's people ballik naked over ler!'

Here's me, 'Lis is a friggin nudist beach, chum. Have ya nat noticed Dean an Dawn?'

Here's her, 'I noticed Dawn like, she's some figure hasn't she?'

Here's me, 'Nie don't you be goin all lesbo on me in a fuckin nudists' beach, chum!'

Here's her, 'No, no. Just sayin like.' Nen, sure doesn't Dean stand in front a us wih his schlong about level wih our faces. Sure I tried til stare at his knee an Big Sally-Ann put her sunglasses on. Sure it was skunderballs like. Here's him, 'I'm goin over to get some ice-creams here – yous want one?'

Here's Big Sally-Ann, 'Awye, thanks.'

Nen here's him, 'What about you Maggie, you want a poke?'

Sure, I coulden help it, I bust out laughin right intil his nads. Here's me, 'Any closer an I'll be gettin a poke in le eye by thon, chum,' an I pointed at his Wilbert. Here's him, 'Is this your first time at a naturist beach, girls? Come on, don't be shy now.'

Here's me, 'Awye, chum … we'll get used til it.' Nen he sauntered off til le wee café hut, wih his arse chewin chewin gum. Sure I didden know what til do. Scarper back til our hotel or get blacked an lose my inhi-bini-bitions. Nen I thought, Mr Red White and Blue's at le hotel an I didden wanna see him at all after le night before … so I gat out le battle a rum. Big Sally-Ann musta had le same idea, cos she lifted le battle a fizzy wine, an we clinked battles an started swiggin.

Well, I'm tellin ya, bein in le heat must do somethin til your ability til cope wih drink cos me an Big Sally-Ann were blootered within half an hour. Dean an Dawn were sittin tellin us all about ler naturist lives an all. Sure ler's nudist places in Norn Iorn – can ya believe it? Some wee place near Ballynure actually lets lem do naked horse ridin an all! Woulden mind goin up ler myself some time an doin a Lady Godiva.

Sinead an Mickey had gat out of le water in le nip, carryin ler swim costumes – but lat didden surprise me. Sure lemens were two hornballs like. But Dean an Dawn said it wasn't about sex

– it was about bein free an all. So, sure Big Sally-
Ann stands up an starts singin, 'I am what I am,
I am my own special creation …' Nen she rolls
down her bikini battams an does a wee twirl.

Nen here bes me, 'Special all right, chum. Ley
broke le mould when ley made you!' An we all
pished ourselves laughin. But sure I was next, I
just thought, ack frig it. Sure who knows ye? So,
I wallaped le lat off an run down til le sea wih
Big Sally-Ann chasin me. Sure I was lat busy
luckin over my shoulder at her boundin toward
me like a big dopey Labrador, I missed my
footin, tripped on a sandcastle some twat had
built, an fell face first intil le sand. Big Sally-Ann
len tripped over me an went flyin head first intil
le sea. Pure shambles. Sure I cud hear Sinead an
all in stitches laughin at le heck of us an I was
just about til get up when I hears, 'Margaret –
are you ok?'

Here's me, 'Ah fuck.'

I lucked up an sure it was Mr Red White and
Blue … an I was bare-arsed an lyin face down
in le sand.

'Margaret – can I help you up?'

Here's me, 'No! An why aren't you naked

– lis is a nudist beach!' Sure I was skundered. Nen he just says, 'Sorry, sorry.' An carries on walkin along le shore. Big Sally-Ann saw what happened – here's her, 'Maggot, mon in da hell. Fuck him!' So, I gat up an staggered intil le sea. Like no matter hie far I went from thon hotel, I still coulden get away from him. Sure I was ragin about it.

Big Sally-Ann went til get le blow-up lilos til cheer me up. So, we sat at le edge of le sea, ballik naked an blowin up a massive cracadile an whale. But, I'm tellin ya, see wih le drink an le sun – an len puffin an blowin for half an hour, le two of us was near faintin. Len Big Sally-Ann says til me, 'Fuck me Maggot, luck at lem two comin along le beach.' So, I lucks round an ler's lis god an goddess strollin along hand in hand. Sure le girl was like somethin outta *High School Musical* – blonde, all-over tan an glow-in-le-dark teeth. But yer man … Jaysus yer man. I've never seen a schlong as long as thon. It was near down til his knee. Here bes me til Big Sally-Ann, 'No wonder she's smilin, chum – ya cud play golf wih his middle leg!' An she started titterin – here's her, 'I'm sure he'd get a hole in one!'

So, le closer ley gat, le harder it was til luck away. Big Sally-Ann starts talkin jibberish, just til talk about somethin. Nen as ley reach us, a big wave rushes up an splashes us. Sure yer man an woman just luck at us an smile an sure here bes me, 'Lat was a big one wasn't it?' til le woman. Well, she didden know what til say. I think she thought I was talkin about King Kong's ding-dong. Sure I tuck a redner. Big Sally-Ann was skundered too. She was laughin lat much she coulden contain herself so she lifted her blow-up whale an run intil le waves wih it. So I fallied her in. An we had a pure geg messin about on blow-up lilos, ballik naked in le sea. Pure beezer like.

12

An ice-cream slider an a cuckoo cock

Well, later on lat day me an Big Sally-Ann had decided til have a wee snooze on le beach. Big Sally-Ann woke me up askin if I wanted another poke so I says, 'Awye will.' I was kinda semi-canscious an I was dreamin about Mr Red White and Blue an me in le sea, havin a severe touchy-feely-no-putty-inny. Nen I feels my face goin cool, like it was bein shaded an all. So, I opened one eye. Nen I let a yell outta me an sat up. Sure ler was some auld lad standin over me. No joke, he was about ninety. Here's me, 'Whaaa?'

Here's him, 'Hi there, how are you da-day?'

Here's me, 'Eh … great, chum.' Sure I cud tell

98

by his accent he was American. Nen I rubbed my eyes an tuck a better luck at him. Jaysus, he was a nudist too. He'd long grey curly hair, wih a fishin hat plopped on top an a camera hangin round his neck – it was stickin out cos of his swollen beer belly – an nen I lucked under le belly. An water belched intil my mouth. All I cud see was a mass of grey fluff where his dick was supposed til be. An lis wee browny-grey shrivelled thing stuck in le middle. Like a chestnut mushroom.

Here's him, 'Nice day for it!' Nen he stares at le Muff an here's him, 'Ah ...' – nen he points at it – 'I like that natural look ... are you European?'

Here's me, 'Belfastian like.' Nen I lucks round an Big Sally-Ann's nowhere til be seen. But I notice lat le ice-cream hut is shakin violently. Here's me til myself, fuck she must have asked for a slider. Nen yer man does a big stretch, pushin his arms up intil le air an yawnin. Well, le wee chestnut mushroom popped out from le fluff when he stretched, an len when he put his arms back down, it went back in again. It was like a cuckoo cock.

Nen here bes him, 'Ahhh. Here's my wife.' Well, lis auld doll came danderin up from le sea like Jabba le Hut. She'd long grey hair … in fuckin pigtails. Here's me, 'Whaaa?' She dandered over an outstretched her hand, 'Hi there, Monica.' She bent over til shake my hand an I swear her nipple touched her knee. Nen here bes le auld lad, 'She doesn't speak English, Monica … European.' Nen he points at le Muff again.

Here's me, 'Excuse me, chum – I do speak English. I said Belfast – like in Norn Iron?' Nen I started feelin around for my sarong til cover myself. Like I gat what Dean an Dawn were on about – like about feelin free an all. But ley weren't all like lat. Le nudist beach was like a pervy bastard paradise. Nen Monica says, 'Oh yes! We have Irish relations.'

Here's me, 'Donchas all, chum.'

Here's her, 'Yes, that's it Donegal, right?' Nen she shakes her towel an says, 'This is a nice spot, mind if we sit here?' An she didden wait for me til say, 'Fackaway off.' She just put her towel down on le sand right in front of me. Nen, she tuck out her suncream, bent over an started rubbin it on her ankles. Her hole was about two foot away from my face. Here's me, 'Whaaa?'

Thon crack was deeper lan le Grand Canyon. Here bes me, 'Ack, I'm a bit burnt – have til go sit in le shade nie like.'

Nen yer man says, 'Ouch. You want some cream for your breasts, darlin?' Nen I lucked down an le baps were like walnuts nie. Nen he tuck le suncream an poured it intil his hands an came towards me. Here's me, 'Howl yer horses, chum. Put lem hands anywhere near me an I'll bounce ye up an down thon beach by le pubes.' An he tuck a step back, 'Sarry, sarry ... tryin to help.'

Here's me, 'Why doncha help yer wife suncream her ankles before her hole swallies up le whole of le Costa Blanca.' Nen I grabbed our stuff an run towards le ice-cream hut.

Well, it was empty, but I heard gigglin an Big Sally-Ann sayin, 'Give us a lick a yer lallipap!' So, I went round le back an opened le door. Big Sally-Ann was lyin on le floor wih ice cream on her diddies an a fuckin flake in her clout. I says til her, 'Chum, did ya nat learn a lesson from le other night?' Len she quickly tuck it out ... an le wee ice-cream man put it back in le bax a flakes on le counter. Here's me til myself, I hope thon

Yank gat lat one. Pervo.

Well, me an Big Sally-Ann dandered back til le hotel – we were both shattered. Sinead, Mickey, Dawn an Dean were all in le water when le Yanks came over so we left lem ler. Back at le hotel, we finally gat til meet Reuben, le rep. An sure wasn't he from Belfast! Here's him, 'Ack I'm sarry, loves. Yer bags is nat here yet – pure lost like!' Sure he was as camp as Christmas … but pure lush like.

Here's me, 'Like lis isn't good enough, chum. We've been wearin lese T-shirts since we gat here … an we've two pair a knickers between us.' He screwed his wee face up an here's him, 'Ley'll turn up. Ler's a laundrette service in le hotel – let me get yer clothes washed for yez complimentary. All right?'

So, we hoofed it back til our rooms, shoved all our clothes in a beg an give lem til le wee porter boy. So, seein as we'd nat a stitch til wear, we gat intil bed an had a wee doze.

Well, our clothes were delivered tip-tap. All clean, smellin fresh – an even our knickers were ironed. Big Sally-Ann an me had gat lem printed before we went. Hers said 'Get 'er Bucked' on le

102

front an mine said 'Muffalicious.'

Here bes me, 'Right, big girl, let's get our flamenco dresses on an hit le town le night ... after we've drunk le bar downstairs dry – right?'

Here's her, 'Awye like! I'm dyin til have a good rummage about down thon bars an all.'

So, we gat le gladregs on, an headed down til le restaurant for a feed. I caught Mr Red White and Blue's eye on my way til get seconds. He was sittin at a table wih Deirdre-No-Diddies an le two of lem were a picture of misery. She'd a couple a lettuce leaves on her plate an a cherry tomata an he'd a half-eaten bowl of pasta. Here's me til myself, fuck ley sure know hie til live. Sure what's le point atein pasta an salad when ya've every kinda food ya can imagine ler at yer fingertips! So, I piles my plate full of steaks, chicken wings an roast potatoes. Len I poured a dollop a gravy over le lat an sauntered past lem. Sure, I was tryin my best til push him outta my mind. Cos, I knew deep down lat he was no good like. But when he looked at me, sure my lips quivered ... an I don't mean le ones on my face.

Anyhie, Sinead an Mickey came down an I

telled lem all about le big Yank an his cuckoo cock. Sure ley were in stitches. Nen Big Sally-Ann tells lem about her gettin a slider in le ice-cream hut. Nen here bes Sinead, 'Well, here, we'd better go. We're goin out wih Dean an Dawn le night. A couples' party.'

Here's me, 'A couples' party? What do ya mean?' Nen it clicks. Sinead lucks down at le table an Mickey starts whistlin at le wall. Here's me, 'Yez are goin til a nudist party aren't yez?' Nen Sinead busts out laughin an here's her, 'Awye! Pure geg. Do yous nat wanna come?'

Here's me, 'No thanks, chum ... I had enough of grey-pubed pervos le day. Me an le big girl's gonna go out hoorin an tourin on le town le night, aren't we, chum?' Big Sally-Ann was deep in thought, here's her, 'Dawn's lovely, isn't she?'

Here's me, 'Oh frig, she's goin all *Prisoner Cell Black H* again. See yez le marra sure, chums.' Nen Big Sally-Ann elbowed me an started laughin.

So, after dinner, we went til le wee bar an gat tanked on rum an cokes an cacktails. Sergio Andre an Craig Diego were a bit put out lat we were goin out on le town an nat goin til le staff do after hours like. But we didden go on haliday til go steady wih le locals. We wanted til give our flaps a bit of an airin like. I fancied a bit of Frankfurt an Big Sally-Ann was gaggin for a British banger.

Ler was a wee do on in le hotel, an it was a drag queen mimin til Shirley Bassey an doin some jokes. It was good craic like. But when le drag queen tuck a break, Big Sally-Ann walked across le stage til go for a slash an le lights went up an she gat a big cheer. Sure, le crowds thought she was le start of act two an she was a big tranny! Sure I coulden stap laughin like. She run along le stage shoutin, 'I'm a woman, I'm a woman! Yez shar a shites, yez!' An some fella shouted out from le audience, 'Course you are!' An she gat another big cheer. So, she didden come out of le toilets for ages. I was sittin decidin what cacktail til get next when I gets a tap on le shoulder. I turned round an it was him. Mr Red White and Blue. Here's me, 'Are you fallyin me like?' An he lucks all shifty an all.

Here's him, 'I don't want it to be awkward between us, Margaret. I'm sorry about last night. I couldn't help myself. But I'll try to avoid you from now on. I see that you are having a great time with your friends and I don't want to spoil that for you. You deserve to have fun.' Nen he smiled at me an sure le Muff was frothin like a Buck's Fizz. Here's me, 'Right will.' Nen he danders off. An ya wanna seen his arse ... sure he'd gat chino shorts from somewhere. He must have a share in Dunnes Stores or somethin, le amount a chinos thon big lawd owns. He was like an Adonis wih his tan an his twinkly eyes. Ya know one a lem fellas lat just goes dark brown if he is in le sun for like ten seconds? Like Big Billy Scriven tuck me down til Crawfordsburn a few months ago an it was scaldin. He went bright red an len by le time we gat home he was white again. An lat's what most Belfastians are like. Us an le Scottish. All Celts alike. Well, nat really ... le Scots are worse lan us. Ler was a wee girl from Glasgow in our hotel and she was actually a shade of green. God bless her. But I telled myself, 'No, Maggie, no. Remember what he did til you.' So, I cancentrated on le cacktail list. Le wee waiter came up an says, 'Yes lady what can I get you?'

Here's me, 'I'll have a Slingapore Sing please ... an one for ma friend.' Nen he just laughed an started mixin it up. Nen I lucked round an Mr Red White and Blue had gone. Prabably back til Deirdre-No-Diddies til rub aftersun intil one of her backs. So, I sighed an says til le waiter, 'Make us six a lem, chum ... an two straws.' I decided lat I needed til get pure full ... an get down lat town an pull somebady just as gorgeous, smart an sexy as Mr Red White and Blue.

13

Gimme yer big meaty molecule, Professor Cox!

Well. After le big girl gat outta le bogs til another big cheer, we bolted an headed for le town. We decided to do a bar crawl … cos like none of le two of us cud hardly walk. Lem cacktails taste like juice but see when le fresh air hits ya, yer proper poleaxed like. We went intil an English pub called Le Red Lion but sure ler was football on le big TVs an none of le wee lawds give us a second luck. So we went intil one a lem cabaret bars – Rockerfellas. Cos like ler was seats an we needed til sit down before we fell down. Big Sally-Ann ordered us two jugs of sangria an ya wanna seen le size a lem. Ler was bits a fruit floatin around on le tap – like we never gat lat at our hotel. Ley scrimp on le extras when it's free drink ya know. Well, here's me til le big girl, 'Don't you be atein lat fruit or your arse'll be on fire in le mornin!' Like, I remember le time we went til le Christmas Market down le town an she tuck a couple a pints of strawberry beer from Germany … sure she ended up in le Portaloo for le rest of le night. Just as well ler was a wee brass band playin til drown out le gurglin noises comin from her arse! Anythin at all foreign in her an she's done for...

'But I'm starvin, Maggot!'

Here's me, 'Whaaa? Chum you ate a piece of steak le size of a rhino about two hours ago!' But nathin wud satisfy her. She started atein le fruit.

Here's her, 'It's only strawberries an grapes an all … like what harm can it do?'

Anyhie, we sat an watched some of le wee acts lat were on, an ley were a geg! Ler was a Roy Chubby Brown-like comedian, drag queens dressed as le Spice Girls an a Elvis tribute act. Le sangria was flowin an we were havin a belter laugh like. Elvis even came over til our table an we gat our photies tuck wih him an all. But he wasn't too impressed when I flashed my baps in le photie – sure I had my arm round his neck at le time an his cheek was against my left walnut. Well, le later le night, le more raunchy le acts gat. We musta been on our tenth jug of sangria when on came … Long Schlong Silver. Sure we'd seen him in Benidorm le last time we were ler an Big Sally-Ann had ended up gettin us threw outta le bar cos she squirted suncream all over him.

Here's me, 'Nie big girl … settle yerself.'

Here's her, 'Oh isn't he gorgeous! Luck at his hair an all.' Sure he was a Chippendale wannabe, long hair, white teeth an built like a brick shithouse. Like he'd some rack on him. Muscles galore, smothered in baby oil. But a bit too womanly for me wih le long hair an all. Sure I like lem a bit rough, so I do.

Well as soon as Long Schlong Silver started dancin til 'Sex Bomb', Big Sally-Ann cud take no more. She danced from her seat up til le dancefloor an he welcomed her on til le middle of le floor. He musta forgat her from before. Well, he was dressed like a soldier in camouflage, wih an army hat an all on. He tuck his sunglasses off an put lem on Big Sally-Ann len he made her sit on a chair in le middle of

110

le dancefloor. Sure she was lovin it. She shouts over til me, 'Fuck, it's like bein up in Girwood barracks again!' An I laughed, rememberin hie we'd scaled le wall of le wee army barracks down le Crumlin Road one time an ended up in a wee tin hut thing wih a bunch a soldiers an all. Sure we brought a couple a battles a Buckey in wih us an none a lem had tasted it before. So sure us bein dead on, we shared it wih lem. Sure ley ended up pure snattered an strippin off for us an all. I bucked one a lem on le tap bunk an Big Sally-Ann done two or three of lem in le battam. Nen ler boss came in an we gat threw out. Said we coulda been arrested an all. Spoilsport. Big Sally-Ann loves a man in uniform like – an so do I. Soldiers, firemen, peelers, binmen, vicars, lallipap men, le lat.

Well, Long Schlong Silver whacked off his shirt an straddled her on le chair. Len he grabbed her hands an trailed lem up an down his chest. Len he gat up an sat on her knee, facin me. An he grabbed her hand an shoved it down his trousers! Well Big Sally-Ann lucked at me round his shoulder an she give me a thumbs up an shouted, 'Tent pole, chum!' An le crowd bust out laughin. But here Long Schlong Silver didden like it cos he wanted til be centre of attention. So, he ripped off his trousers an gat a union jack fleg an wrapped it round himself. Len he tuck off his thong an flicked it at Big Sally-Ann. An she put it on her head. Len he started walkin round le crowd flickin his dick under le fleg. Sure didden Big Sally-Ann start singin 'le Sash', an le crowd was wettin lemselves at her. So, Long Schlong Silver went over til her an made her lie on le floor. Nen he stood over her an squatted on her face! Sure I near died. Here's me, 'Whaaa? What's he doin?' But le next thing Big Sally-Ann sat up an she had his tallywhacker in her gob! Well, he jumped back in shack an ended up slippin on le oil on le floor an fallin down on til le dancefloor himself. So, Big Sally-Ann tuck advantage of le situation. She straddled him. An although he was Mr Muscle, he coulden shift le big girl. He tried til wrestle her til le left and til le right, but he was no match for her. Sure she was twenty stone of pure Belfast beef sittin on tappa him. Well, she did a bit of space-happin on him before two security guards trailed her off, nen she came back til le table.

Here's me, 'Fair play til ya, big girl! Ya near had him ler.'

Here's her, 'A did have him, a wee bit went in – sure I pulled my knickers til le side!'

Here's me, 'Whaaa? Ya semi-bucked Long Schlong Silver! Legend!' Nen we clinked glasses an decided til go an get praper boys at one of le nightclubs.

Well, we were lat blacked lat we went intil le wee nightclub across le street an lumbered le first wee lawds lat we fell on. Sure ley were sittin at le bar drinkin pure oranges. I think ley are what le youngens call 'geek chic' – ley had glasses on an I think maybe anoraks. I was lat blacked I coulden tell. So me an Big Sally-Ann telled lem ley had til come til le beach for a touchy-feely-no-putty-inny an I think ley were too afeared til say no. So, ley came. Big Sally-Ann's boy was tellin her about hie le sea was polluted in Benidorm an she was all ears. But I saw her lickin her lips too an I thinks til myself, thon wee lawd's nat gonna know what end of him's up in le mornin.

My boy was all intil le stars an le universe an all. He pointed out le Pegasus shape an says it

113

was a constellation, an lat we coulden passably be le only life in le universe. Sure I thought I was wih Professor Brian Cox an I was near dead til de-beg le wee lawd. Oh Jaysus I love Professor Brian Cox like. An I'm nat exaggeratin. I actually love him. Le way he says 'stars' an 'molecule' an all just makes me wanna rub le Muff across his lips. Nie I'm nat one of his new fans an all since he's all smart an on TV an all. I've loved him since le time he was in Kelly's in D:Ream, singin 'Things Can Only Get Better' in 1992. Sure everybady was after Peter, le lead singer, but I had my eye on big Brian from le word go. Ack, he knacked me back like when I tried til trail him intil le bogs when he came off le stage, but I forgave him. An I've loved him since len. So, I was hangin on my wee geek's every word an cos I coulden see straight, I cud pretend it really was big Brian Cox when I was buckin him. I was all biz.

Nen le wee geek lucks up at le sky an says, 'Look! There's le frying pan!' Nen, I farted an here's me, 'Ler's an egg til put in it, chum … nie commere til I get a luck at your big dipper …' An I trailed him on til le sand an on til a sunlounger.

Well, I wrecked thon wee lawd. Sure I was callin him 'Brian' in le middle a buckin him. I was shoutin, 'Oh Brian, oh Brian, give me your big meaty molecule!' An he was sayin, 'Um, my name's Derek.'

Here's me, 'Talk stars to me, tell me about le Milky Way!'

Here's him, 'Well, it's milky.'

Here's me, 'It sure is, chum – keep on pumpin ler!'

Sure it was pure beezer. We all dandered up from le beach an gat dirty kebabs from a wee street stall. Big Sally-Ann had broke her fella's glasses when she sat on his face. An when he was gettin stuck intil his doner kebab, she whispered, 'Remind you of anything?' An winked at him. Here's me, 'Fuck sake, big girl, ya've put me off mine nie!' So, me an her sauntered back up le dirt track an intil our beds.

Here bes me, 'Lat was some night, chum, but le marra it's down til business. We've til buy as much fegs as passible wih le money we've left all right?' But le big girl was already snorin, so I closed my eyes an joined her.

14

Takin advantage of le free table tennis ... table

Well, le next day, we didden get up til near thee a'clack. An sure we'd missed breakfast an lunch. Big Sally-Ann was pure ragin like cos see if she doesn't get her food, she turns intil le Hulk. So, we flung our sarongs on over our bikinis an headed down le town til get some grub. Lucky for us, most of Benidorm were also hung over til fuck an all le wee bars an all serve breakfasts all day. Sure we gat a fry for two quid each, which was just as well cos we were runnin outta money, fast. Big Sally-Ann had just ordered a pavalova an here's me, 'Fuck sake, chum, where do ya put it? Pavalova for breakfast?'

Here's her, 'Ack, I'm still growin, chum …
ya don't get a figure like mine without some
serious atein!' Nen she grabbed one a her bellies
an give it a wee shake. She's nat wise. So, while
she was atein her pavalova, I gat our money out
an counted it all out. Here's me, 'Jaysus, chum,
we've spent loads. We're nat gonna make any
prafit at all on lis haliday by le time we pay yer
da back what we barrowed.'

Here's her, 'Frig it must have been all lem
sangrias an all.'

Here's me, 'Awye. From nie on, we'll have til
get blacked for free at our hotel an nen get fellas
til buy us drinks down le town, right?' So, we
sauntered down til le wee tabacca shap til get
our fegs.

Well here. Le price of le fegs had went up all
right. An nat a wee bit like I'd thought. Sure ley
were near double le price lat ley'd been a couple
of years ago. Here's me, 'Whaaa?' Le wee man
lat owned le shap told me lat his business was
near bust cos nobady hardly came on feg runs
nie lat ley were so dear an all. But sure what cud
I do? I spent le rest of our money on le fegs, bar
a few euros for emergencies.

Here bes Big Sally-Ann, 'Sure worst comes to worst, we can just smoke ourselves stupid, til we're high as kites.' So, on le way back til le hotel, we decides til stop at a bar an get a pint each. Like we were sweltered in le heat an carryin begs fulla fegs. An lat counted as an emergency. So, we were sittin downin le pints when a wee man rolled up on one a lem mobile scooter thingies lat auld people go til le shaps on. Sure ya wanna a seen it, it was sparkly red wih go-faster stripes on le side an all! Here's me, 'Whaaa?'

Here's Big Sally-Ann, 'Frig, Maggot, we cud do wih one a lem til get us back til le hotel wih lese fegs.'

Here's me, 'My thoughts exactly, chum … you distract him while I load it up.' So, Big Sally-Ann went over til le auld lad an started talkin til him an I started til pile le begs of fegs on til le sides of it. Nen sure le buck eejit comes out arm in arm wih le auld lad! Here's her, 'Maggot it's all right, Bernard's gonna give us a lift wih le fegs – he's dead on, chum.' An wee Bernard winks at me an here's me til myself, oh Bernard thinks he's in for a ménage a three here for givin us a lift. But anyway, I jumped on le front an Big Sally-Ann an Bernard jumped on behind me. I turned round an le big girl was sittin on his knee. Sure ya cud hardly see him behind her – he was a wee fart like Ronnie Corbett. So, off we went. Like it was goin dead slow – about a mile a decade – wih all le weight on le back. But still, better lan walkin. I was cancentrain on nat runnin anybady over, but it was hard. Le chatterin an giggles an all from behind was distractin me. So, I turned round til tell Big Sally-Ann til shut up an sure wee Bernard was clingin on til her … by le diddies. Here's me, 'Whaaa?' But she just winked at me an says, 'Ride on, Maggot!'

Well, when we gat til le hotel, wee Bernard wanted til buy us a drink – but we telled him it was all for free. Nen Big Sally-Ann offered til get him a free one for givin us a lift an all an he says aye til lat. Here's me, 'I'm away up til le room wih lese fegs, chum … see yez at le bar.' An sure as I was walkin off I hears wee Bernard sayin til Big Sally-Ann, 'So, tell me more about the free table tennis.'

Well, on le way up til le room, I bumped intil Sinead an Mickey. Sure ley were ravin about le nudist party. Here bes Sinead, 'Ya wanna seen it.

Le men were pure gorgeous – not a grey pube in sight like.'

Here's Mickey, 'Awye le women were like catwalk madals too. I bucked three like.'

Here's me, 'Whaaa?'

Here's Sinead, 'Ack it's all right ... me an Mickey are havin an "open" relationship.'

Here's Mickey, 'Awye, she opens her legs til anybady nie!' Nen Sinead dug him in le ribs an he staggered off down le hall laughin. Here bes me, 'You sure yer up for lat, chum? Like seein Mickey buckin other women an all?'

Here's her, 'I wasn't watchin ... I was busy lumberin le bake of some big ride from Australia, chum! We're goin back again le night. You shud come, chum! It's great craic like!'

Here's me, 'Frig I might!' Nen she run til catch up wih Mickey. An I thinks til myself, like, I never thought Sinead wud be intil lat like. Len, I thought about Mr Red White and Blue an I wondered if he really had changed. An nen le door knacked. Here's me, 'God's sake where's your contin key, woman?' But when I answered it, it wasn't Big Sally-Ann. It was Mr Red White and Blue.

Here's me, 'Hie did ya find out my room number?'

Here's him, 'Margaret, I can't stop thinking about you. I … I … I don't know what to do.'

Here's me, 'Where's Deirdre-No-Diddies?'

Here's him, 'Tummy bug. She's in the apartment. Can I come in? There's things I want to say to you.' Well, I tried wih all my might til shut le door in his face, or tell him til fack away off. But I coulden. I opened le door wide an he walked right back intil my life again.

'Margaret. I know you won't believe me, but I've changed. After you left me that day, I looked at myself long and hard and I knew I had to change. I did it for you, but you wouldn't take my calls and then I realised that you were too good for me.' Nen he hung his head down in shame.

Here's me til myself, I'm too good for him? Does he really think lat? Nen he takes my hands in his and pulls me towards him an he says, 'Margaret. Tell me now. If you've no feelings for me at all, I'll walk out the door and you'll never see or hear from me again. But if you think about me sometimes and you wish that things were different then …' Well, I tuck one luck at his wee twinkly eyes an his wee sexy lips, an I jumped him. Like literally, jumped up intil his arms an wrapped my legs around his waist. An he lumbered le bake clean off me. He run intil le bedroom wih me wrapped round him an he flung me down on le bed, 'Oh Margaret.' I untied my sarong an he ripped off my bikini, nen, he slowly tuck his chino shorts off an his schlong sprung forward an here's me, 'Oh, I've missed you.' An he says, 'And I you.'

Nen here's me, 'I was talkin til yer wab, chum.' An before I cud say, 'Get 'er bucked,' he was ridin le life outta me. Nie, I was half expectin him til start tyin me up, or whippin me wih somethin, but he didden. It was buckin, pure an simple.

Nen after, we lay on le bed, luckin out le open doors til le balcony. Le sun was settin an le sky was reds and oranges. An I wished lat le moment wud never end. Nen, he says he has til go but asks me til meet him later on, after dinner. So, I told him til come til le room an I'd be ler. Sure I knew lat Big Sally-Ann wud wanna go til le nudists' party wih Sinead an Mickey … so we cud have le place til ourselves. Like I felt a bit guilty about Deirdre-No-Diddies, cos like I don't like buckin men lat are spoken for – I do have morals. But like she stole him from me in le first place. Nen, after he left, I went out til le balcony an lucked across le sea. But I gat distracted, I thought I heard somebady whisperin my name. Nen I bent over le balcony an I saw her. Through a skylight below, I saw Big Sally-Ann lyin on le table tennis table. I cud only see her from le waist up. But by le way she was bein thrust up le table, I knew she was gettin rid. Here bes her, 'Be up in a minute … I can smell chicken! Fuckin starving, chum!' Nen she waved at me. Nen she lucked down towards her feet an says, 'Bernard, get a move on, will ye?'

I decided nat til tell Big Sally-Ann about Mr Red White and Blue. Cos like I knew what she'd say. An I didden wanna hear it. I wud tell her lat I wasn't well an was goin til bed an she shud go on out wih le rest of lem. So, I flung on my Peter Andre T-shirt an dandered down til le restaurant til lie til my best mate.

15

Le burnin bush

Big Sally-Ann was chewin on a rack of ribs when I telled her. Here's her, 'Ack Maggot – it's nat like you! You always go out when you're nat well!' Sinead an Mickey were too busy lumberin le bake off each other at le table til comment.

Nen here's me, 'Ack, I think it's le auld age creepin up on me – I can't hack it like I used til.'

Nen here bes her, 'Okay will. Oh here, did I tell ya I had le skitters after lat fruit last night, chum? Ya were right, I shouldn't have ate it. Sure I had til finish Bernard off wih a blowie while I was on le bog down in le sports room.'

Here's me, 'Fuck a duck, lat's what I call multi-taskin, chum.'

Nen here's her, 'Frig, luck ler's yer man from

le Bru atein on his own.' An she pointed over my shoulder and ler he was, sittin luckin at us – nen he put his head down when we all lucked over.

Here's me, 'Buck eejit.' An I tried nat til make eye cantact wih anybady.

Here's Big Sally-Ann, 'Fuck maybe he's drowned Deirdre-No-Diddies in le bath an buried her bady in le sand!' Nen she bust out laughin an I was glad I'd decided nat til tell her I was gonna be ridin him within le hour.

Here bes Sinead, 'Sure you come wih us Sally-Ann – it's a geg like. Ley've big bowls of punch an ya can buck all round ye.'

Here's Big Sally-Ann, 'Ack I'll maybe just stay wih Maggie. Like it's bad craic leavin her on her own an all.'

Here's me, 'Nooooo! No, chum. You go on, I'd rather just go asleep, an you'll only do my bax in, keepin me up talkin shite an all.'

Nen here's Sinead, 'Awye, Sally-Ann … leave her til it.' Nen she winked at me an I thinks, she knows what I'm up til. Ya can get nathin by thon wee Sinead I'm tellin ya. She's no dozer, like.

So, after Big Sally-Ann had finished off her third chocolate mousse, we dandered out til le reception. We'd telled Sergio Andre lat we weren't goin til le do again, cos I was sick an all. But we never said lat Big Sally-Ann was goin til ride all round her at le nudists' party. Dean an Dawn arrived an Big Sally-Ann was all biz. Nen off ley went intil le night, an I run upstairs til get ready. Like, I knew lat no matter what Mr Red White and Blue said, he still was intil bondage an all. Like lat wud never change. Once a hornball, always a hornball. But ler's a fine line between lat an batein le tripe outta somebady. So, til show I was up for a bidda rough, I nicked a couple of bits of bamboo off a plant in le hallway. Nen, I made le bed for le first time since we gat ler, an I ripped one of le pilla cases up intil long bits, so he cud tie me up an all. An like just le thought of it had me drippin like a leaky tap.

I had a shower, put on my red lipstick an my 'Muffalicious' knickers. I decided til just wear le knickers, an surprise him. Len le door knacked. I bolted til it … len I waited for a few seconds – so nat til luck too keen an all. Nen I flung it open an stood ler wih my diddies stuck out like a proud pigeon.

'I knew it! I fuckin knew it! Who is it? Yer

man from le Bru?' It was Wee Sinead. I trailed her in an here's me, 'Awye. But don't be tellin Big Sally-Ann … she doesn't like him. An I'm nat sure lat I'm gonna buck him yet.'

Here's her, 'Awye, ya don't luck like yer gonna buck him him all right!' Nen she bust out laughin, 'Luck, I'm nat here til spoil yer fun. I wanted til give ya lese …'

Here's me, 'Whaaa?' In her hand was couple of blue pills an a wee pink tub lat said 'Pussy Rub' on it. Here's me, 'What in le name a God?'

Here's her, 'Ack, I brought lese wih me for me an Mickey. Here…' An she put lem intil my hand.

Here's me, 'I take it lis rub isn't for yer cat len?'

Here's her, 'Maggie ya have til try it, it's pure beezer. Put a bit on yer Muff before ya do it an ya'll be squealin le place down, chum.'

Here's me, 'Right. An what's lese pills? I'm nat wantin til get off my face nie!'

Here's her, 'No, it's like Viagra but for women. Sure I need it til keep up wih Mickey – he ates Viagra like ley're smarties, fuck sake!' Nen I realised why ley were at it morning, noon an night.

Here's me, 'Stickin out, chum! Thanks like!' Nen she high-fived me an away she went. So, I said til myself, fuck it, ya only live once. So, I tuck one of le pills an rubbed a bidda le stuff on le Muff. An len le door knacked ∴ an it was him.

Well, as soon as I opened le door, le cream started til work on le Muff – sure it was on fire! It was like lat time Big Billy Scriven went downtown on me after atein a kebab an chilli sauce. Mr Red White and Blue smiled at me, lat wicked smile lat telled me I was gonna get pummelled, an instead of sayin 'Hiya' I said 'Sweet Jesus Christ le night!' an my knees went. Mr Red White and Blue grabbed me an led me til le bed. Here's him, 'Margaret, what's wrong? Are you feeling faint?' Nen, I telled him about le rub an he suddenly went all quiet. Here's him, 'Margaret … you have sticks here … and ripped sheets. Are you telling me something?'

Here's me, 'Chum, ya'd better get inda me quick, my Muff's like le burnin bush.'

Well, he grabbed le ripped sheets an tied my hands behind my back. Len he rolled me over an tickled my arse wih le stick – an he gave it a few whips as well. An I was on fire.

Here's me, 'Quick! Buck me quick!'

But he just laughed an rolled me over, an here's him, 'Margaret – you really are something else.' Nen, he jumped on me, an away we went. Nie I dunno if it was le blue pill, or le Muff rub or just le thought of Mr Red White and Blue ballik naked – but I was Bell again, ding-a-lingin like Big Ben on New Year's Eve. He had me every way in le book for three hours. His stamina was unreal. Like when he had me from behind, I was hangin over le balcony, an he had my legs under his arms like I was a wheelbarra. An I thinks til myself, one shove nie an I'm tatey bread like. But I trusted lat he didden actually wanna murder me. Maybe he had changed … Nen after, we were lyin on le bed, an I asked him where Deirdre-No-Diddies thought he was. Here's him, 'I said I was going for a walk; that I needed air.'

Here's me, 'For three hours? An did she nat mind you leavin her sick an all?'

Here's him, 'Let's not ruin it by talking about her.' Nen he kissed me an I run my hand over his rack-hard bare arse, an I pushed le wee feelin of uneasiness lat I had about le whole Deirdre thing right til le back of my mind, as he ravished me for le second time.

Well, we planned til meet le next day down at le beach. I knew Big Sally-Ann wud fall asleep after bein out buckin and gettin blacked all night, so I cud sneak away. He said he'd be watchin me from afar, an when I went intil le sea, he'd swim out an meet me.

I was asleep when Big Sally-Ann came in from le nudists party. I heard her stumblin about in le dark, fartin an len flappin down in le bed. An she was snorin within seconds. So, I just left her til it an went on til dream about Mr Red White and Blue an me gettin married on le beach.

16

A Muff dive in le Med!

Well. Le next day, I woke up early. Well, it was about ten a'clack an lat's early for me. All le buckin an no drink le night before seemed til give me a wee spring of life like. I was fulla beans. I tried til roll Big Sally-Ann out of bed, but she wasn't for movin. She stank a festered drink – hanast til God, it woulda knacked ye out. So, I shoved my sarong on an run down til Sinead's room, til see if ley were up. I knacked for about ten minutes nen said til myself, ack frig it, I'll go on down for breakfast myself. Like I was feelin all brave. Cos like ler's nathin as sad as sittin atein on yer own, surrounded by happy couples an all.

So, I went down til le restaurant an had a luck

around. I spatted a table lat was big enough for about eight people – in a wee alcove part. So, seein as ler was no wee tables free, I just went an sat ler. I cud see eyes fallowin me, women feelin sarry for me, or feelin skundered for me atein on my own, or a bidda both. Nen I lucked at some of le berks ley were sittin wih, an I felt like sayin, 'Don't feel sarry for me, chum – luck at le Shrek luckalike lat you wake up til every mornin!' But I said nathin. I just plonked my beach beg down on le table an went up til get some grub.

Well, I was ravenous – like le 'after sex' munchies had only started when I woke up. An hanast til God, I coulda matched Big Sally-Ann lat mornin in an atein competition. So, I lifted fried eggs, bacon, sausages an beans an I went til go put some toast in le wee toaster thingy. Like I cud hardly wait for it til go round le wee conveyor belt. So, when some big German woman tried til nick my bits of toast, I coulda killed her stone dead ler an len. Here's me, 'Here, Helga! Don't think so, chum!' Nen she lucked at me like she didden speak English so here's me, 'Nien!' An I lifted my toast an she starts shoutin some German intil my bake. But here's me til myself, I'm too starvin til start a ruckus. So I just smiled an said, 'Two words, love. Winston Churchill.' Nen I dandered off til my table.

Well, I was gettin wired intil my breakfast when Craig Diego comes over wih a coffee pat. Here's him, 'Lady, I havth not seen you. You go away an leave me?'

Here's me, 'Ack, love, I'm in demand – what can I say?' Nen he just laughs an fills my coffee cup up.

But in my head I was thinkin, he may be a buckball, but he's no match for Mr Red White and Blue. I tuck a sip of my coffee an remembered Mr Red White and Blue untyin my hands le night before so I cud give him a good grope. Nen I hears a voice, 'Margaret – why are you alone?' An I opens my eyes an he's standin ler in front a me.

Here's me, 'Whaaa? Chum I only have til think of you an you appear before me in a puff a smoke!' Nen he just smiles an I says, 'Ley're all in bed. Ley were out at a nudist party last night – all blacked an bucked senseless.'

Nen here's him, 'I don't want other men

looking at you naked, Margaret. I don't want you to go to the nudist beach again.'

Here's me, 'Awye.' Like, I thought til myself, ack lat's a normal reaction from a fella til nat want other men oglin yer flange on a beach like. But ler was a wee flicker of le old Mr Red White and Blue in his voice lat I didden like.

Here bes him, 'Seeing as they're not around, shall I join you?' So, he went an gat his breakfast an sat down at my table. I glanced around at le couple of women lat had lucked at me wih pity, an ley were now starin at me wih daggers ... pure jealous of le big ride sittin next til me.

He had two bits of brown toast an fruit on his plate. Here's me, 'Whaaa? Luck at all le free food on offer here an you're on le fruit, chum?'

Here's him, 'I look after myself, Margaret.' Nen he gat stuck intil a peach. Well, sure I was watchin his mouth as he sucked an slurped it an all I cud think about was him doin lat til le Muff. Sure he hadn't had a munch on me le night before cos of le Pussy Rub an all. So, I was gaggin for it, an so was le Muff. I was near in a trance watchin le peach juice drippin down his chin. Nen he lifted a watermelon an gat stuck intil lat, an sure I coulden take my eyes off his mouth. I'd a fanny like le end of a Prit-stick, I tell ya – sure I was near enough stuck til le wee seat I was sittin on.

Here's him, 'You're staring at me, Margaret.'

Here's me, 'Sarry, sarry.' An I lucked away. Nen he tuck my hand an says, 'Margaret, are you biting your lip? You know what will be going on in my shorts right now, don't you?' Well, I was pantin like a horndog. I dove under le table, unzipped his flies an had a good auld go on his Blackpool Rock. An as I was smokin le bone I cud still hear him rammin his face intil le watermelon an bits were fallin outta his mouth an on til my bake – sure it was pure dirt an I was lovin it.

Well, when he started scrapin le innards of le watermelon wih his tongue, I cud take it no more. I slid up from under le table an near ate his face off. He knew what I wanted, an was happy til oblige. He tuck me by le hand, an run me out til le beach. But we coulden find anywhere secluded. Le place was full of kids an all. Nen I spatted le pedalos. Here's me, 'Lese will do.' So, we jumped on an started pedallin out til sea.

Well, I was gaggin for it lat much, I was goin like an Olympian til get as far out as passible. My thighs were on fire wih le strain, sure I hadn't done any exercise since Gorgeous Gavin le lifeguard started le aerobics class down in le Grove swimmers. Sure, we all joined up til get a luck at him in his vest an shorts, but he turned up in a full tracksuit an made us all actually do all le fitness an all! Didn't go back like.

Well, after pedallin out about a mile, we stapped. No words were said. Le excitement of it all was too much like. I bounced outta le seat, an jumped intil le back of le pedalo. I'd whipped off my bikini by le time Mr Red White and Blue joined me. Here's him, 'Oh Margaret, you're … you're …'

Here's me, 'I'm friggin spittin love-juice here. Get yer snorkel on, chum – lis is gonna be le Muff dive of yer life!' An it was – sure he was at it ages like. I was lyin back on le pedalo wih le sun kissin my diddies while he lapped it up down below. Sure I lost count hie many times I bolted like. I lost all sense of where I was, cos le boat was gently rockin an all, an it was sendin me intil a wee daze. Nen, I feels le rockin gettin a bit more hardcore, an len le pedalo was like shakin from side til side. So, I opens one eye an lucked behind me, an le beach was like miles away, an we'd drifted out til sea! But if lat wasn't bad enough, I felt my whole bady get shaded. An I turned round … an ler was a fuckin cruise ship le size of le *Titanic* right beside us. Here's me, 'Whaaa?' An I jumped up. An I heard gasps an all as all le people lat were hangin over le handlebars watchin us seen my bake for le first time. Talk about a redner! Me an Mr Red White and Blue jumped intil le drivin seats of le pedalo, an peddled back til le shore laughin our balls off.

Well, when we gat back in, we gat off le pedalo an kissed cheerio on le beach. I was sure Deirdre wud be luckin for him, an Big Sally-Ann wud be up an luckin fed. So, he rushed off in one direction, an I walked slowly in le other. An I was just thinkin about comin clean til Big Sally-Ann when I hears, 'You've scarred lem cruise ship wankers for life, Maggot.' An I lucks up an ler, sittin on a sunbed, wih her binoculars, was Big Sally-Ann.

17

You tellin me ya rimmed Chesney Hawkes?

Well. It turned out she'd been on le balcony, hangin her knickers out til dry, when she'd seen me an Mr Red White and Blue gettin intil le pedalo.

Here's her, 'I knew ya were meetin him last night Maggot. You never turn down a party. Even lat time ya had le mumps an lucked like Sloth from le Goonies, ya still went til le karaoke in le Rangers Club.'

Here's me, 'But why didden ya say anything?'

Len she sighed, 'I thought ya cud tell me in yer own time, chum.' Nen I felt terrible lat I'd lied til my best chum like. So, I said sarry, an she said

138

it was all right. Nen, I sat an told her everything. An God love her, even though I knew she hated him, she said she hoped it all worked out an all.

'But if he messes about wih you again, Maggot, I'll drop-kick le cont, an stick him on le spit-roast in le restaurant.'

Here's me, 'All right, will.'

Well, lat night, I went out wih Big Sally-Ann an Sinead an Mickey. Like I coulden take Mr Red White and Blue out wih my mates – I knew ley woulden get on. Ley were like different breeds an wud clash – I just knew it. An I felt wick buckin him when he was on haliday wih another woman. Even though she'd totey diddies, an he was bound til stray. I saw him at le restaurant – he was on his own again.

Here's me, 'Where's Two-Backs?'

Here's him, 'Still ill.'

I nodded, 'Oh right. Maybe see ya when I get back?'

He sighed, 'Maybe.' An I cud tell lat he was a bit pissed off lat I was goin out wih my mates, an nat stayin in wih him. But like I was Miss Piggy-in-le-middle. All I knew was lat I wasn't gonna ditch Big Sally-Ann, no matter what. So, we gat blacked in le hotel before headin down le town til Sinatra's Bar. Craig Diego was sniffin round some new arrivals lat had arrived an I says til myself, ack fair play til him. Like ya can have too much of a good thing like. An it wud get him off my back too. Big Sally-Ann had lost interest in Sergio Andre too since she'd met Franq le German at le nudists party. Jaysus she didden shut up about him. He was six-foot-seven wih a dick like a snow shovel. Every woman at le nudist party was luckin a go on him but he picked Big Sally-Ann. Here bes her, 'He says he likes a big woman. Nen he headbutted my diddies an says he wanted til wrestle me!'

Here's me, 'Whaaa?'

Lis is her, 'Awye! So we had a wrestle out on le patio, an when I gat le better of him, sure his middle leg shot up like a jack-in-ma-bax!'

Here's me, 'Get it inda ye!'

She laughed, 'A did!' An we all bust out laughin. So, he'd telled her lat he'd see her in one of le bars lat night, an she was near-dead til see him. Lat is until le next act came on in Sinatra's. Le wee host fella belted out, 'And now, ladies, gents an ladyboys! The moment

you've been waiting for! It's the one and only ...
Chesney Hawkes!'

Here's me, 'Whaaa?'

Here's Big Sally-Ann, 'Fuck me, a Chesney
Hawkes tribute – oh I'm gonna faint so I am!'
An we all watched le dancefloor wih our mouths
hangin open. But it wasn't a Chesney Hawkes
tribute act. Oh no. Not in Benidorm. It was
le fuckin REAL Chesney Hawkes! Sure he
sauntered out on til le middle of le floor wih his
blonde locks an his wee mole an all an shouted
on le mic, 'Benidorm are you ready?' Well, me an
Big Sally-Ann exchanged lucks an we shouts
tilgether, 'YEEEOOOOOWWWWWWWW!'

Sure me an Big Sally-Ann pure love Chesney
Hawkes. Like we went all le way down til
Newcastle til le Radio One Roadshow in 1990
til see him. We'd our hairs done in spiral perms
wih Sun-In sprayed on til make us more blonde,
an our baggy jeans an red LA Gear guddies
on. We thought we were just le dogs' like. We
gat right til le front of le crowd, after Big Sally-
Ann decked a couple a spides outta le way. Like
nobady wud of tuck le big girl on – even in lem
days she was a six-footer. Well, Big Chesney

came on, an I swear he lucked at me … right in le eye. Len he run down past le crowd, high-fivin everybady. But when he gat til Big Sally-Ann, she clung on til his wrist wih all her might. Sure he was a pro like an carried on singin til one a le bouncers came an put her arm up her back til she let go. Nen when he went off stage an intil le Slieve Donard, we fallied him! Bounced past le security guard, an run about le rooms luckin him. But len we lucked out one a le windees, an saw lat a helicapter had come til take him away! So, we run outta le hotel an down til le beach, but as we gat ler, le helicapter lifted off up intil le air. So, sure, didden we run intil le water after him. Like he waved down at us, an lat was enough for us. He noticed us! Like we were neck deep in le sea in our clothes but sure. Felt like dicks sittin watchin Right Said Fred like wih our jeans soaked an weighin ten stone a pair. Ack, but it was one of le best days of summer … like ever.

Here's Big Sally-Ann when Chesney started til sing, 'Remember Newcastle, Maggot?'

Here's me, 'Was just thinkin about it, chum!'

Here's her, 'Corner him in le bogs after he's done?'

142

Here's me, 'Ya read my mind, chum.' So, we sneakied backstage. Here's me, 'I'm gettin first lumber.'

She shoved me outta le way, 'No, me!' An as we were squabblin, sure out he came, all breathless an all. I think he thought we worked ler, cos he asked Big Sally-Ann for a glass of water. So, she went til get him one, an I moved in for le kill. Here bes me, 'Oh, I've loved you since 1990!' An I jumped him. Like, he put up a bit of a fight, but I still gat a lumber in.

He squealed, 'I'm married!'

Here's me, 'I'll make an exception lis time!' Nen I tried til lumber him again. But a wee bouncer had seen le commotion, an trailed me off him. Big Sally-Ann came danderin over wih a glass of water, an le bouncer escorted le two of us outta le place.

Here's me, 'I snogged Chesney Hawkes!'

Here's Big Sally-Ann, 'Well, I licked his glass round le rim.'

Here's me, 'You tellin me ya rimmed Chesney Hawkes? Legend!' An we both wet ourselves laughin.

Well, le night gat very messy. Big Sally-Ann

gat stood up by Franq le German, so she was on le pull again. Le last thing I remember was dancin til 'Le Soldier's Song' in a wee Irish pub wih Sinead an Mickey while Big Sally-Ann was singin 'Le Fields of Rathenrie' til a wee lad from Drogheda. Sure it was bedlam!

18

FLABBA

Well. Le next mornin, I woke up in bed til find Big Sally-Ann standin over me, near nose-til-nose. Here's me, 'Whaaa?'

Here's her, 'Maggot – yer bake!' Well, I sat up an rubbed my eyes. I was still steamin from le night before. Nen I lucked at her an here's me, 'Ma bake whaaa?' Nen I noticed somethin black on her face. So, I rubbed my eyes again an squinted at her. Well, she'd marker pen drawn all over her face. But she was pointin at me – here's her, 'Ye've gat pen all over yer face, chum!' Here's me til myself, oh no. Len, le memories of le night before slowly flooded back til me.

We'd been harrassin a wee waiter in le Irish bar. He'd a marker an notebook for takin big orders … cos like ley know hie much le Irish can drink in Benidorm. So, we tuck le pen off him an drew 'rent boy' on his forehead. Like he was up for it an all, thought we were a geg like. But len me an her gat carried away wih le pen.

Big Sally-Ann had 'sleg' wrote on one cheek, an 'bitch' on le other, an a fuckin star on her forehead – like Wonder Woman. I bolted til le bathroom an lucked in le mirra. I had 'millbeg' on one cheek an 'hoor' on le other … an a fuckin dick drew on my forehead. Here's me, 'Whaaa?' I grabbed le flannel an started scrubbin le big dick on my forehead. But it wasn't for movin. Big Sally-Ann bust out laughin when she saw her reflection in le mirra.

Here bes her, 'Ack, it's nat lat bad!'

Here's me, 'Nat lat bad? Yer nat le one wih a penis on yer coupan, chum! What's Mr Red White and Blue gonna say?' An it was outta me before I even had a chance til think about what I was sayin.

Here bes Big Sally-Ann, 'Who gives a fuck what he says, Maggot? Don't you be lettin him change you an all again, chum.'

Here bes me, 'A won't.' But, I already felt that

I was tryin til please him too much.

Well, Big Sally-Ann went down til breakfast wih Sinead an Mickey, an she brought me up a doggy beg. Two well-done steaks, a chicken crown, an a basket a chips. An I scoffed le lat. Len Big Sally-Ann went down til sunbathe, an I said I wud stay in le room til le wee cleaner came. Sure I thought she might have somethin til take le pen off my bake like. So, while I was waitin, I decided til luck at le feg situation, an I wished I hadn't. Sure we only had enough fegs til break even … we weren't gonna make any money at all. An if we carried on spendin le way we were, we woulden even have enough til pay Big Sally-Ann's da back what we barrowed. I was ragin. Nen, I hears a knack at le door an I shouts, 'Who is it?'

'Margaret, it's me. Are you okay? I didn't see you at lunch.'

It was Mr Red, White an Blue. Here's me, 'Nat well, chum … musta ate somethin dodgy.' Sure I didden wanna let him in wih me luckin like somebady outta Ward 10.

Here's him, 'Margaret, I know about your face. I saw your friend Sally-Ann.' Here's me til myself, I'll deck lat wee girl! So, I let him in. Well. Ya wanna seen le luck on his face when he saw me. He lucked at me le way all lemens down in le Bru luck at me … like I'm a bidda dog shite on ler shoe. An I felt skunderation on another level like. Nen he telled me lat I shouldn't go out of le room til it was removed. An I feels like sayin, ya don't have til tell me lat! He was stompin about le room in a bad mood. So, I thinks til myself, well ler's no point wastin a free room is ler? So, I said I was gonna take a shower, nen I winked at him, drapped my robe an strutted intil le bathroom like a catwalk madal – a ballik-naked one.

Well, he tuck le bait. He was straight in after me. He lathered me up wih le soap, an I did le same til him. Nen we had a slippy-dippy ride up against le bathroom wall. Sure it was pure slide 'n' ride amazeballs. Nen he telled me til get on le beeday. So, I did, thinkin til myself, hie le fuck is he gonna buck me on lis! But it wasn't a buck he was after. He went an gat le belt from my robe an tied my hands behind my back.

Well, he leaned down, an I thought I was gonna get a munchin like le day before. But, it wasn't lat. He lifted Big Sally-Ann's razor from le side of le bath an started til shave le Muff.

Here's me, 'Nooooooooooo!' But he skimmed le razor across le Muff like he was a Turkish barber an, within minutes, le whole lat was gone. Here bes him, 'You look like a lady now, Margaret.'

Here's me, 'I'm nat a lady … I coulden give a flyin fuck about bein a lady! Ye've tuck my Muff away! I didden want a baldy coot!' But he just laughed like it was no big deal … but I was ragin. I didden like le luck in his eye when he was doin it, an le luck of victory after it was done. But I still telled myself lat he had changed … like besides a few wee slaps, he hadn't bathered wih all le batein an all. He really hadn't like. An if he wanted til do it, he wud have … I knew lat for sure. I think he musta knew I was a bit pissed off like. Cos he telled me lat buckin wud be different wih a baldy snatch … nen he laid me on le bed an give it til me. Well, I was on all fours on le bed wih him behind me when le wee cleaner walked in. I dunno if it was le big dick drew on my head, or le man hangin outta le back of me, but she screamed an run out.

Mr Red White and Blue run intil le bathroom an put his chinos on, nen he said he'd have til get back to Deirdre if le cleaners were round.

Here's me, 'Whaaa?' But he run out le door. An before I cud ask him what he was on about, another wee cleaner came in, an I showed her my forehead. She laughed an brought a wee battle a stuff in for me. It seemed like she'd seen it done before … but she didden speak a word of English. Like I was a bit worried about le skull's head an all on la battle, but I wanted le writin off, so I near tuck a layer of skin off scrubbin it. An after about two hours my face was clean.

Big Sally-Ann done le same wih hers when she came up from le pool, an we were set for another night on le town. I didden tell Big Sally-Ann about le money situation, cos I didden wanna spoil her fun like. We all met at le restaurant at dinner an discussed where we were goin lat night. I coulden get le worry about le money outta my head, an I was distracted.

Here bes Mickey, 'Well, ler's a karaoke campatation down in Le Black Chicken – sure we cud go down ler an watch people makin conts outta lemselves?'

Here's me, 'A campatition? What's le prize?'

Here's him, 'Five-hunderd euros – can ya believe it? Might even enter myself!'

Here bes Big Sally-Ann, 'Oh Maggot – we cud do "Summer Nights" tilgether!'

Here's me, 'No, nat here – everybady'll be doin lat. We'd need til think up somethin beezer til win like.' Sure, I knew I had til win le campatation til get some money back for us. So, we bolted down til Le Black Chicken bar til eye up la talent an see what we were gonna do.

Well, on le way down til le bar, we passed one a lem wee shaps lat sell le hen night stuff an all. It was called Mr Brightside's an sure wasn't le big fella lat owned it from Belfast! Here's me, 'Whaaa?' Sure I telled him my predicament, an he says he wud help us win le karaoke campatation. Ya called him Big Iain – sure he was a six-footer an Big Sally-Ann was fallyin him about le shap like a wee lap dog.

Here bes me, 'Listen big girl, lis is serious nie. We need til win lis campatation. Listen til Big Iain an stap pervin over him!'

Well, Big Iain came out wih a long blonde wig an a curly brown one. An silver catsuits wih platforms an all. Here's me, 'Whaaa?'

Here's him, 'ABBA! Yas can do "Waterloo" or a medley or "Dancing Queen"! Asides from that, these are the only extra-large costumes I have.' Nen I thinks about it an here's me, 'Lat's nat a bad idea ...' So, we bargained him down on le price, an off we tratted til le karaoke, dressed as ABBA. Like I had til trail Big Sally-Ann outta le shap cos she wanted til buy neon leg warmers an all.

Well, le costumes were a tight fit til say le least. Big Sally-Ann's flares were up round her shins, an I had til undo my zip down til my belly button til let myself breathe. So, le chebs were half hangin out. Here bes me til Big Sally-Ann, 'Right. Let's get blacked. We'll do "Dancin Queen" but a different version – like le way ley do on Le X-Facter. We'll rap it ... an we'll call ourselves FLABBA.'

Here's her, 'Awye. Sure when people see le trouble we've went til, ley'll vote for us like.'

But here, it wasn't as simple as lat. Some wee hoor from England wih fake diddies gat up an done a SuBo. Sure she started singin some song from *Les Misérables* an had all le grannies in le audience gernin an all. Nen, she was hangin off le DJ le rest of le night, like she was near dry humpin him. Me an Big Sally-Ann started on le sangria again … an by le time it was our turn, we were half cut. I tried my best til outdo le SuBo hoor. We rapped le lyrics an Big Sally-Ann flung her hands out every nie an again like le big gangsta rappers in America do, an I tried til do some break-dance moves. But when I flung my leg up in le middle of le song, my costume ripped at le crotch. An sure wih all le buckin an scrubbin my bake all day I hadn't time til wash an dry my only pair a kacks … so I'd none on. Well, I lucked down from le stage an sure I'd flashed my gash til a wee family from Scatland. Le kids were traumatised an cryin an le da was pissin himself. Sure wih le Muff shaved off an all, ley'd gat a pure eyeful of my giblets an everything. My bake was a pure beamer – like my ears an all were bright red.

Sinead an Mickey done Sonny an Cher 'I Gat You Babe.' Ack, it was sickly sweet like. Ya woulden have guessed ley were swingin le night before. Nen it was time til announce le winner. An nobady was shacked lat le wee tart version of

SuBo won. Me an Big Sally-Ann were like batein bears about it. We'd wasted money on costumes … for nathin.

But it turned out a good enough night. Big Sally-Ann found Franq le German an I met a wee fella from Glasgow. We all went down til le beach til do a skinny dip. Like I was still a bit ragin about Mr Red White and Blue shavin my Muff off. So I thought, frig it. He's probably buckin Deirdre anyway. So, we flung our ABBA outfits off an run intil le water like *Baywatch* babes.

19

Neville gets exposed

Well, me an Big Sally-Ann woke up le next mornin on le beach. I cud tell it was early cos ler was birds jumpin up an down on le sand, luckin til ate any grub left behind from le night before. I smiled, rememberin gettin intil le sea naked an shoutin out, 'My fanbax is freezin!' An my wee Scatchie fella tellin me he'd warm it up. Like wih no hairs on le Muff at all, it was feelin le cold more lan before! Nen I hears somebady whilstlin a wee tune an I sits up, an two shells fall off my nips on til my knee. Here's me, 'Whaaa?' Nen I realises lat I haven't a stitch on! I lucked beside me an Big Sally-Ann was le same. She'd two shells on her nips an a clump a seaweed on her clunge. I lucked round an le wee pedalo man was settin out le sunbeds an all – here bes him, 'Good morning, lady!' Nen he winked at me.

Well, I near shuck le life outta le big girl til wake her up. We found our ABBA costumes lyin on up le beach, so we had til run til get lem wih our hands over our fannys an all. Here bes me when we gat back til le hotel room, 'What le hell happened last night, chum?'

Here bes her, 'Le wee Spanian tramp lat we met in le street came down til play us some tunes on his wee banjo job, an sure we lit a wee campfire an danced around it in le buff!'

Here's me, 'Oh awye, lat's right.' An le memories came floodin back til me. Sure I was belly dancin for le wee Scatchie an all. I was lat poleaxed, I forgat what country I was in. Last thing I remember was him ridin me in le sand, an his phone ringin. An le frigger answered it! Nie, lat's nat le first time lat's happened til me. Sure one time I was in my Uncle Marty's flat, buckin a wee soldier from Girwood when his phone went. Sure he telled me he had til answer it, cos he was on call an all. Like lat was in le middle of le Troubles, like, an I thought he was like dead important. But sure when he answered le phone, he went white. He was sayin, 'Oh God, oh God. No, no.' An I was thinkin a massive bomb had went off somewhere or somethin. Len he puts his phone down an just lucks at me, An here was me, 'What's happened – have ye til go an save people an be a hero an all?'

Nen here was him, 'That was my mum back home … my cat just died.' Nen, he started til cry. Sure it was pure uncomfortable! Le buck eejit was cryin about his pussy an he was still in mine!

But anyhie, le wee Scatchie just hung up, an carried on wih me so I was all biz.

Anyhie, seein as it was our last day til sunbathe, we hit le beach. We plastered ourselves in factor zero tannin oil cos we wanted til get burnt til a crisp for goin home. Big Sally-Ann was eyein up le talent wih her binoculars. Here's me, 'Chum are you nat shagged out yet like? Ye've done some ridin lis haliday!'

Here's her, 'Ack ya have til get your hole on le last night, chum. It's le law.' An I was just wonderin if I wud see Mr Red White and Blue on le last night when she says, 'Chum, I noticed last night, yer Muff's away. Did ya do lat for

Mr Red White and Blue like?'

Here's me, 'Awye ... but I'm growin it back like.' She just nodded an I felt wick. Cos like I knew she was thinkin I was a mug for gettin back wih him. Nat long after lat, Sinead an Mickey came down til le beach. Here bes Sinead, 'Here Maggie, yer man was hangin about our corridor luckin ye like.'

Here's me, 'Who? Mr Red White and Blue?'

She laughed, 'Awye. He's an oddball like. Why didden he just knack yer door instead a hangin about?'

Nen Big Sally-Ann pipes up, 'Cos he's been fallyin her wherever she goes, lat's why.'

Here's me, 'Whaaa?'

Here's her, 'Awye, hie do ya think he knows where you are all le time? Like he just turns up out of le blue an all ...' Nen I gat til thinkin like he did just turn up in a puff of smoke all le time.

Here's me, 'Naaaaaa, chum. He woulden do lat. Sure he's here wih Two-Backs remember? Naaaa.' But what she said unsettled me like. An I says til myself, I'm gonna have it out wih him about lat when I see him.

Well, I didden have long til wait. We were

down havin dinner when I saw him sittin wih Deirdre-No-Diddies. Le restaurant was bunged. Most of le people, like us, were goin home le next day, an were stuffin lemselves stupid wih le grub before ley went back home til one pork chap an two scoops a mash again. Me an Big Sally-Ann were at le buffet pickin our second desserts. I was just liftin a slab of chocolate cake le size of a house when Deirdre-No-Diddies appeared. Big Sally-Ann nudged me an I nodded. We hadn't seen her near le whole haliday. She lucked even skinnier lan before an was kinda failed-luckin too. She leaned across til lift a single grape an as she did, her cardigan slid up her arm. Well, I near died. Her arm was black an blue le whole way up. Big Sally-Ann gasped, an Deirdre drapped her grape. Len she pulled her sleeve down in a panic, an started til walk away. Well, I bounced. I grabbed her by le other arm an she let a yelp outta her. I pulled up her sleeve – it was black and blue wih bruises too.

Here's her, 'Please don't.' An she started til cry. Nen I lucked at her face, an her left eye was swollen, like it had been bruised but faded, an she had a faint blue line across le front of her neck.

Well, a volcano of sisterhood exploded in me, an my eyes filled wih fire. I twirled round til where he was sittin an glared at him. His eyes were wide an he was luckin round le room for exit routes. But he wasn't quick enough for me. I trailed Deirdre over til his table, an I went ballistic.

'You rattan, filthy, Disturbia bastard! Luck what ye've done til lis wee girl!' I pulled Deirdre closer an held her arms out. She was proper cryin.

'Margaret, this is not the time, or the place for …'

Here's me, 'Oh is lat right? Oh let's keep up le act lat you're a decent fella in front of everybady will we, *Neville*? Let's nat let everybady know what a complete cont you are!' Well, by lat time, le whole restaurant had gone silent. Nat one person even dared til chew in case ley missed a bit of le action.

Here's me, 'You've been buckin me le whole week an tellin me you've changed – holdin back, tryin til be normal. Len you were goin up til le room til bate le life outta Deirdre! Ya fucked up bastard!' He tried til mumble somethin, but I didden let him. I shoved my fist intil his gob. Len, I lifted his plate of pasta, an I poured it over le tap of his head.

Here's me, 'Nie, get back til whatever gutter you came from. I may shout an drink an be a so-called millbeg an like havin a full bush ... but I wud NEVER treat another person like a dog le way you do. Ya hate women, hate lem! Yer a sleekit cont an a woman-batein bastard!'

Well, he gat up from le table, an he run outta le place. I lucked round an everybady was sittin glued til me til see what I was gonna say next. Big Sally-Ann winked at me, an she started til clap slowly. Nen others joined in. Nen le whole place was clappin an cheerin.

We tuck Deirdre up til our room, an let her have a shower. Big Sally-Ann sat down on le bed, 'Is lat his name? Neville? I never heard you callin him lat before.'

Here's me, 'He doesn't deserve til be Mr Red White and Blue no more. He's just Neville. Sadistic cont, Neville.'

Well, when Deirdre came outta le shower in a towel, we seen le full scale of what he'd done til her. Ler were bruises all over her back, whip marks an all – an some had near broke le skin. I cud hardly luck at her. I says I was goin til le balcony for a feg, while Big Sally-Ann put some Sudocrem on her. But I needed to get outta ler. I stood on le balcony smokin a feg, an I cried my heart out. How cud a man do lat til a wee woman like Deirdre? Like she was so tiny an feeble. An he'd made out til me lat she was a nutcase when it was him was le nutcase all along. I felt awful lat I'd been sucked in by him again. I'd let myself down good an praper. But I cud put it right. I dried my eyes an went back intil le room.

Here's me, 'Right. Sally-Ann, ring down til reception. Tell le hotel manager til get up here nie wih a master key. Deirdre, stick lat Peter Andre T-shirt on, chum. We're goin til your room tilgether til get your stuff, an you're stayin in our room le night. Ya can come home wih us le marra too.'

She lucked at me an I swear ya cud see in her eyes lat she'd been broken. Here bes her, 'Why are you doing this for me? You hate me.'

Here's me, 'Nansense. Us girls have til stick tilgether, chum. Especially against a vicious bastard like him.' An she cracked a wee smile, an I put my arm around her, 'Mon, get le T-shirt on ye before le manager sees ye like lis.'

Well, it was Craig Diego lat came til le door wih le master key. Here's him, 'What is wrong? Have you lost a key, lady?'

Here's me, 'No, chum. Lis wee girl here's been attacked by her fella. We want til go til her room an get her stuff – her passport an all.' He lucked at Deirdre an nodded.

Well, when we gat there, Neville was away. Le room was like a dunderin-in – completely trashed. He'd left in a hurry. An le bastard had tuck Deirdre's passport wih him. Still tryin til control her til le last minute. We gat le wee rep Reuben til come up til le room, an telled him everything. An he sat an held Deirdre's hand while he telled her what he cud do. He was gonna apply til le embassy for a copy passport, but it wud take a few days. An Deirdre hadn't a penny til stay on at le hotel nor nathin cos Neville had tuck le lat wih him.

Here's me, 'I'll sort le bill, chum. Reuben, you do what ya have til.'

Well. We tuck some of Deirdre's clothes back til our room, an Big Sally-Ann says, 'Right. What we need is a girlie night out. Drink, dancin an men.'

Nen here's Deirdre, 'Maybe not the men?' An we all bust out laughin. Like in times like lat, sometimes ya have til laugh or ya'd cry. So, lem two gat busy gettin ready in le bedroom, while I went til get le money til help Deirdre. Like we had hardly anythin left ourselves. Ler was only one way til get le cash. Le wee man at le tabacca shap tuck most of le fegs back, an give me back le money. After I'd telled him le whole story about Neville an Deirdre an all. Thank God there's some decent wee spuds in le world like him.

So, lat was her sorted. Len, on le way back, I was passin Mr Brightside's shap an I thinks, aah fuck it, ya only live once. So, I went in an bought three outfits. Small, large an extra-extra large pink neon taffeta skirts, leg warmers, sunglasses an silver sparkly wigs. Pure beezer like. An I tratted back til le hotel ready for le last night of our halidays.

20

Le sun sets on le Feg Run haliday. Ack. ☹

Well. Me, Big Sally-Ann an Deirdre hit le town like an illuminous tornado. We put our hairs in side pony-tails an all like in *Grease* – sure we lucked le part like. Deirdre turned down le pink tutu, but she put a bidda lipstick on an she didden luck half bad. I thought til myself, it's gonna take a while for thon wee girl til get over what's happened til her here. An I cursed that fucker again.

I'd paid til keep our room on for Deirdre for another four nights. Craig Diego gat le manager til give me a good deal, cos of le situation an all. So, we spent le last of our euros on sangria.

Once Deirdre was pished (after two glasses) she opened up til us about Neville. Sure he'd kept her handcuffed til le radiator, whipped le life outta her, woulden let her wear her bikini nor nathin. I knew len why he run back til his room when he knew le cleaners were goin round. He didden want any of lem til walk in an find her bein kept a prisoner. Poor Deirdre.

We went til Sinatra's an I gat up on til le dancefloor when Long Schlong Silver was on. Big Franq le German had turned up, so Big Sally-Ann was more interested in him lan le stripper. Deirdre's face was a sight when Long Schlong Silver whacked his thong off an bounced his Wilbert in my face. I was glad til see her smilin.

We ended up havin a pure ball lat night. Sinead an Mickey went for one last skinny dip wih Dean an Dawn le nudists. Me, Big Sally-Ann an Deirdre went til a wee quieter bar on le outskirts of le town an Franq's mates were all ler. We telled lem we were fluent in Irish an all an it was a pure geg. Sure we telled lem lat 'No surrender' meant 'Hello' an lat 'Diddy ride' meant 'I like you.' Ya wanna hear lem all sayin

'No surrender' in ler German accents – it was pure beezer like.

Nen one a lem came an sat beside me. Ya called him Rudolf – but he gat Rudi for short – on account of all le reindeer jokes an all.

Here's him, 'Vat is your name?'

Here's me, 'I'm Conny. Conny Lingus… pleased til meet you.' An I shuck his hand.

Here's him, 'Conny Lingus … ah I like it.'

Here's me, 'I bet ya do, chum!' An I tuck him for a wee walk down til le beach til find out just hie much he did like it.

Well, we were gettin picked up by le coach at six a'clack in le mornin, so we decided nat til go asleep. Deirdre had went on back til le room, seein as she was stayin an extra few days. Craig Diego walked her back up in case ballbeg was hangin about waitin on her. I cud see by le way he was luckin at her, he was after a goodnight kiss. Ack, I didden mind like. She deserved til get a good ridin from a man lat didden knack her melt in afterwards. Me an Big Sally-Ann went down til le beach an sat an watched le sun come up til le bus arrived.

Here bes Big Sally-Ann, 'Maggot my da's

gonna kill us for spendin all le money.'

Here's me, 'Ano, chum. But we'll pay him back. We'll have til go an beg for our jobs back in le chippy or somethin. Fuckin take us years wih le pittance ley pay like.'

Here's her, 'Ack it'll nat be so bad – wee Bananaman'll keep me company sure.'

Here's me, 'Are ya still after him like?'

Here's her, 'Ack, he's good craic like. Like ya don't have til be buckin him til have a good time. Ya can just sit an talk like. Like we do.'

Here's me, 'Awye. Fuck men like lat are hard til find like.' An nen Big Billy Scriven papped intil my mind. He was a bit like lat. I wondered if he was a daddy yet. An nen a wee picture appeared in my head, as quick as a polaroid. Me an Billy an our wee baby. Nen I shuck it off, an telled Big Sally-Ann all about Rudolf le red-dicked German. Like although we'd had a great time wih le Spanians an Germans an all, ler was nathin like a roll wih a good auld Ulsterman. An we were near dead til get home for an Ulster fry, Tatey cheese an onion an a praper cuppa tea. So, we said bye bye til Benidorm an headed home in our Peter Andre T-shirts … an not a feg between us.

Well, when we touched down in rainy Belfast, it was enough til make ya wanna stow away in le under carriage of le plane til get back til le sun. Even though ya may be suffocated on le way. Reality had hit me. I was gonna get thon baby rubbed in my face at every opportunity by Gretta Grotbegs – I just knew it. We were all waitin for Sinead an Mickey's begs tilgether. Sexy Anthony was waitin for us outside le airport. Len I hears a few people start til giggle, len proper laughter, len somebady done a big belly laugh. I coulden see what le commotion was, cos me an Big Sally-Ann were at le back of le crowds. Sinead papped her head out between two people an here bes her, 'C'mere yous two – mon see lis!'

Well, we pushed an shoved til we gat til le front an ler, comin round le baggage belt, was our begs. But nat only lat, le entire cantents of le begs was all splattered along le belt, on tap of everybady's suitcases. My PVC thongs, my Katie Price bikini, Big Sally-Ann's belly-holdin-in knickers an her wee Rangers teddy bear. It was like a fucked-up version of le *Generation*

Game. We started til grab our stuff, an people were in stitches. Len, le finale. Ler, sittin on tap of a fake Burberry suitcase, was Big Sally-Ann's Rampant Rabbit. An some fucker on le baggage staff had turned it on. Well, le place was in an uproar. An like we had til see le funny side, so we just laughed along wih everybady.

Well, we were tellin Sexy Anthony all about it on le way home. I was dyin til ask was Big Billy's baby born yet, but I didden wanna luck like I give a shit. Big Sally-Ann musta read my mind, cos here bes her, 'Have ya seen Big Billy about?'

Here bes Sexy Anthony, 'Aye, frig sake, he hasn't been outta the Shebeen all week – the baby was born the day yous went.' My heart sank. Lis really was le end.

Nen here bes Sexy Anthony, 'It's black. Not his. Turned out he didn't even buck her. She met him in the kebab shop – he'd passed out drunk. She carried him home, and tried to shag him while he was asleep the dirty blirt! But they didn't do it at all. Feel sorry for him like. He's gutted about it.'

Well, my heart skipped a beat. Big Billy didden cheat on me at all. He was only a stupid bastard, not a cheatin one. Big Sally-Ann nudged me an winked, an I smiled. Le clouds parted as we were drivin along le Hightown Road an le sun beamed down, lightin up le road in front of us. I coulden stap thinkin about Billy le whole way home. I was first til get drapped off an when Sexy Anthony drove intil my street, he started laughin. I lucked out le car windee an ler he was standin at le front door of my black a flats wih a big bunch of flowers. Big Billy Scriven.

Here's Big Sally-Ann, 'Go on ya girl ye!' I gat outta le car an len I seen it. Le buck eejit had somehie painted all over le front of my black a flats. Ley were normally plain white but he had painted red love hearts all over lem. An, ler, between le battam a my flat windee an le tap a Dora Simmonds windee was painted in red, 'Marry me Maggie?'

Here's me, 'What le furry fuck is lis?'

Big Billy held out le flowers an said, 'I'm sarry, Maggie, please forgive me like. It's you … it's always been you.' So, what can a girl do like? I lumbered le bake clean off him ler an len! Sexy Anthony started beepin his horn an all lemens in le car were cheerin an all. So, I give lem le finger an me an Billy went intil my flat. I give him what for like for puttin me through all le shit.

Here bes me, 'Nie don't think lat I was a good girl on haliday – I was buckin all round me, cos you were wih thon swamp donkey.'

Here's him, 'Ano Maggie. I'm sarry – hanast til God, I am.'

Here's me, 'A heard ya were gutted lat le baby wasn't yours?'

Here's him, 'A was Maggie. Ack, a gat used til le idea of it like. A wee nipper runnin about, ya know?'

Here's me, 'An what's Gretta sayin about it all?'

Here's him, 'Ack, she tried til stroke me like Maggie. But I feel sarry for her in a way. I went down til le pram shap and paid off what was owed on le pram an all – give her a bit of a start anyways.'

Here's me, 'You're one of a kind Billy Scriven. Ya'd have been a great daddy too.' An nen I felt about fifteen.

Here's him, 'Maybe one day Maggie. You'd make a great mammy too.'

Nen here bes me, 'Do ya think? Well, ya never know what might happen.' An I smiled at him. An he knew what I was sayin.

Nen here's me, 'Well, ya can kiss me again if ya like.' An I folded my arms an lucked le other way. Len, he came over, grabbed me round le waist, an leaned me right back an kissed me on le lips – like ley do in le auld black-an-white films.

Here's him, 'I missed ye Maggie.'

Here's me, 'Hie much?' Nen he grabbed my hand, an trailed me intil le bedroom.

Here's me, 'Nie I wanna pastie bap outta Beatties an a Tatey crisp sandwich straight after, right?'

Here's him, 'No bather, Maggie, no bather, love.'

And here ... there's more ...

Well, le big confrontation wih Big Sally-Ann's da didden go as badly as we thought it wud. Sure le two of us went round wih our tails between our legs til get le face chewed off us. But turned out it was Big Sally-Ann's da lat was in le dog house. Sure he'd only gone an won ten grand in le bookies – nat le two grand he'd telled us about. Big Sally-Ann's ma had been talkin til wee Gail Russell lat works in le Spar on le Road – sure her da owns le bookies where le bet had been put on. So Big Sally-Ann's ma had went beserk an she made him cough up le rest of le cash, after puttin him on his hoop. An she telled him lat he was nat til ask us for le money back lat we barrowed. It was a present. So lat was us off le hook. Jammy conts like.

Sinead an Mickey broke up when we gat back – but ley still meet nie an again for a buck if ley're fancyin it. An ley meet up wih Dean an Dawn nie an again til go til le nudists' parties lat ley have. Sure Big Sally-Ann went a few times wih Bananaman too – but I think they prefer just buckin each other nie. They're all loved up like. He even gat an estate car so ley can buck all round le place in comfort. She says she's tryin til straighten out his dick once an for all.

We heard from Deirdre-No-Diddies le other day. Sure thon wee doll never did come back from Benidorm. Her an Craig Diego gat tilgether, an ley are openin a wee bar next summer – we're all goin over for a feg run and til see le bar an all. Sure our Will came round wih his laptap an we done a Skype where we cud see lem on le screen an all. Isn't technalagy nie amazeballs? I'm half-expectin Marty McFly til whizz past my windee in a DeLorean one a lese days. Ya wanna see Deirdre nie – ya woulden recognise her. She's her hair long an wavy, dyed blonde, and she wears make up an all. She'd a wee butterfly clip in her hair … an it just reminded me of her – she was like a new person nie … free an all. She'd a lucky escape from thon berk Neville. An so did I.

I heard lat he'd gat le sack from le Bru an I was glad – serves him right. But, in a way, I feel sarry for him. Somethin terrible musta happened til him to fuck him up in such a twisted way. An I hope he cures himself of it somehie, I really do, or it's nat gonna end well for him.

Me? I'm just me. Happy go lucky Maggie. Chancer, mouthpiece an good-time girl. Big Billy's by my side … like he always really has been. Only nie, we're hand in hand. I always said he'd be a great daddy an he will be. Lis Christmas. He wants a boy but I want a girl – ler's enough men ruinin le world wihout another one!

Ya know le other day, we were sittin in Beatties chippy havin an Ulster fry. I was dippin my fried egg intil mustard (weird cravins) an he just lucked at me an smiled. Here's me, 'Whaaa?'

Lis is him, 'Nathin Maggie – just you, just you.' Nen he lifted his fried egg an plapped it down on my plate. It reminded me of le wee bit in *Lady and le Tramp* where Tramp gives Lady his meatball. Len, he stroked my face. An lat says it all chums … says it all.

The End

Acknowledgements

I would like to thank Blackstaff Press for publishing the book, and for their continued support. I would like to thank my family – my mum, dad and sister for babysitting and an honest opinion. Thank you to all the Maggie Muff fans on Facebook who told me their hilarious stories of holidays in Benidorm – some have been used but I'll not tell you which ones! Thanks to my mates who have hardly seen or heard from me in the last few months while I've been scribbling away.

Big thanks to Martin Lynch and GBL Productions who have brought Maggie Muff to life on stage in a fabulous way and to Caroline Curran for playing Maggie so well.

Finally, thanks to all of the Facebookers who have liked, shared and commented on the

'50 Shades of Red White and Blue' page – it's been a crazy journey and I hope you all enjoy the last story in the trilogy! Long live the Muffsta!

Leesa xxx

THE FIRST INSTALMENT IN
MAGGIE MUFF'S ESCAPADES – AND THE
SMASH-HIT BESTSELLER

Fifty Shades
of Red White and Blue

Well. Lis is a wee story about me an Mr Red White
and Blue. Sure didden I meet him
down in le Bru on a back-til-work interview.
He was tall, dark an bucksome– an he
was gorgiz in lem chinos.

So nie if ye want a wee giggle an yer nat too
squeamish, let me tell ye all what happened –
sure ye'll nat believe it. We're talking baps, blindfolds
an a Belfast Bus Tour ye'll never forget.
Oh Mammy, don't start me!

Maggie Muff xx

Paperback – £5.99
ISBN 978-0-85640-905-9

Also available as an eBook – £3.99
EPUB ISBN 978-0-85640-077-3
KINDLE ISBN 978-0-85640-082-7

www.blackstaffpress.com
www.leesaharker.com

THE SECOND INSTALMENT IN
MAGGIE MUFF'S ESCAPADES

in
le Shebeen

Well. It all started when Big Sally-Ann announced
what she wanted for her fortieth birthday. Nat satisfied
wih le two-man tent I gat her for doggin up Black
Mountain, she wanted til do le last dance from
Dirty Dancin in le shebeen on her birthday night.
Here's me, whaaaaaa? Ya wanna hear le carry-on
lat went on tryin til get it all organised.
Big Igor went missin, Big Billy Scriven gat his oats,
I met a wee lawd called Jake-Le-Peg an Wee Sinead
was buckin all round her – shameless!

We're talkin fake passports, front wedgies an a
Zumba class lat I'll never forget. Oh Mammy, don't
start me! Nie, get a wee feg lit an a cuppa tea
(or a pint a Buckey) an I'll tell ya all about it!

Maggie Muff xx

Paperback – £5.99
ISBN 978-0-85640-906-6

Also available as an eBook – £3.99
EPUB ISBN 978-0-85640-144-2
KINDLE ISBN 978-0-85640-162-6